THE VIRGIN WIFE OF A BILLIONAIRE

TANIECE

The Virgin Wife Of A Billionaire

Copyright © 2024 by Taniece

All rights reserved.

Published in the United States of America.

All rights reserved. No part of this publication may be reproduced, distributed, or transmitted in any form or by any means, including photocopying, recording, or other electronic or mechanical methods, without the prior written permission of the publisher, except in the case of brief quotations embodied in critical reviews and certain other noncommercial uses permitted by copyright law. For permission requests, please contact: www.colehartsignature.com

This is a work of fiction. Names, characters, places, and incidents either are the products of the author's imagination or are used fictitiously. Any resemblance of actual persons, living or dead, businesses, companies, events, or locales is entirely coincidental. The publisher does not have any control and does not assume any responsibility for author or third-party websites or their content.

The unauthorized reproduction or distribution of this copyrighted work is a crime punishable by law. No part of the book may be scanned, uploaded to or downloaded from file sharing sites, or distributed in any other way via the Internet or any other means, electronic, or print, without the publisher's permission. Criminal copyright infringement, including infringement without monetary gain, is investigated by the FBI and is punishable by up to five years in federal prison and a fine of $250,000 (www.fbi.gov/ipr/).

This book is licensed for your personal enjoyment only. Thank you for respecting the author's work.

Published by Cole Hart Signature, LLC.

Mailing List

To stay up to date on new releases, plus get information on contests, sneak peeks, and more,

Go To The Website Below...

www.colehartsignature.com

CHAPTER ONE
HONEY HURTS

"Did you ever figure out what we were doing for our twenty-first birthday?" my fraternal twin Coco asked as we crossed the campus of Alabama State, heading toward the Acadome parking lot where the truck was waiting for us. We both were in our third year of college, she studying for her bachelor's in education and I, forensics science. For us to be twins, we were nothing alike. She had the patience to deal with kids but me, not so much. Don't get me wrong, I loved kids, but I couldn't be around some that weren't mine for too long. They irritated the fuck out of me. Coco wanted this big ass family while I, on the other hand, wasn't even certain if I wanted kids.

Crime was my passion. I love true crime. The shit excites me. The thought of working in a lab was my dream. When I found out about Alabama State's forensics program, I couldn't pass that up.

"I haven't really decided yet," I finally answered. We were stuck between throwing a party and just getting on a jet and getting the hell out of here. Coco didn't want the burden of trying to figure out what we were gon' do so she just put it off on me and had been asking questions about it ever since.

"Honey! Coco!" our best friend Marcia called out our names from behind us, and my steps halted. The sun blinded my vision when I turned around. I pulled my Fendi shades down over my eyes and Marcia's beautiful mocha face came into view. My beautiful black Barbie. That's what I referred to her as. Everything about her was just flawless. From her icy smile down to the curve of her hips. My girl could give Jayda Cheaves a run for her money.

"I was hoping I caught y'all before you left. Are y'all coming to the Kappa's party later? I heard it's supposed to be epic."

My eyes darted over to Coco, who tucked her silky, voluminous, spiral-curled auburn hair back behind her ear. Her amber eyes gapped at me.

Turning my attention back to Marcia, I replied, "I don't know. We'll see."

Pressing her hands together, Marcia placed them at her mouth and said, "Please. I really don't want to go by myself."

Out of my peripheral, I saw Coco place her hands into her jacket pocket and purse her lips. Parties weren't really her thing, hence the reason why she kept questioning me about what we were doing for our birthday. She preferred a trip to Greece and call it a day. Me, on the other hand, I'd party my ass off every chance I got. We were young. There was nothing wrong with having a little fun here and there.

"We might show our faces. Just depends on if Coco is done studying."

"I—" Marcia's words were halted with the sound of screeching tires behind us. Coco and I turned around to see a black Sprinter van stop directly in front of us. Two men dressed in all black with ski masks on their faces jumped out. One had an assault rifle strapped to his chest and the other held a shotgun.

My books dropped to my feet. Coco firmly gripped me by the hand and yanked me in her direction.

"Run!" Marcia yelled.

Before my feet were even able to lift from the ground, I was bear hugged from behind. Coco stopped and faced me with a white face. "Just go!" I screamed at her.

"I'm not leaving you!"

"Go!" I ordered, but before she could fully release my hand, the other guy grabbed her as well.

"Help!" Marcia screamed out, gaining several people's attention.

"This ain't got nothing to do with you. I suggest you go," the guy holding me said.

"I'm not leaving them! Let them go!" Marcia yelled back.

"If you want to live, you'll take your ass on." He backed toward the van and placed something over my head. Everything went black. Goosebumps coursed my frame, and my breathing hitched. Something tight wrapped around my wrists, and I winced. Moments later, I was tossed inside the van. A body crashed into me seconds after and light sobs came from beside me.

"Where are you taking us?" I questioned them.

"Shut the fuck up," a masculine voice answered.

I jumped at the sound of the door slamming shut on the van and my heart dropped to the depths of my stomach.

Pow! Pow! Pow!

My eyes expanded. At this point, our body guards had to have realized what was going on and were coming for us.

"I don't want to die," Coco said just above a whisper next to me.

"We're not going to die," I reassured her, even though I

wasn't certain myself. The van jerked and my body tilted into something.

"If it's money you want, we can get that for you. Just let us go," I begged.

"Didn't I tell you to shut the fuck up?"

Beads of sweat formed above my upper lip. My eyes roamed the darkness as I tried to figure out exactly how I was gon' get us out of this mess. My lungs began to swell. *Calm down. If they were about to kill us, they would have done it by now.*

I wasn't certain how long we'd been riding for when the van came to a stop. The door opened and Coco's body was removed from my side.

"Ahhhhhh!" she screamed, and my blood boiled.

I wanted to beat everyone's ass in this fucking van. Coco was the gentle, calm, patient one. I was the oldest by five minutes and felt like it was my duty to protect her, and I have been ever since I could walk. Hands wrapped around my ankles, and I was jerked forward. After planting me on my feet, I was yanked by whatever they used to bind my hands together and my feet began to move.

I stumbled, trying my best to keep up with him when I couldn't see a damn thing. My ears perked, hearing a door open, and then my sneakers squeaked against the floor with every step I took. I walked for what seemed like forever 'til another door opened and whatever was covering my head was yanked from it.

"Honey! Coco!" Ma screamed and lifted from her kneeling position, but the guy standing beside her pushed her back down by the shoulder. Tears streaked her cheeks. Next to her was Daddy on his knees. His bald head shined like brand-new hardwood floors from sweat. Moisture filled his eyes when his head lifted, and our gazes met.

"Wha-what's going on?" I asked them as we were shoved in their direction.

"Sit down," I was instructed and did as I was told with Coco at my side.

My eyes wandered the room we were in. It looked like some form of basement. Saws, machetes, and knifes nested neatly against the wall next to us like wall art. My heart palpitated.

Yeah, they were about to kill us.

"Can somebody please tell me what's going on?"

"Honey, for once, can you just be quiet?" Daddy ordered me, and my head snapped in his direction so fast that I thought I gave myself whiplash. We were in a room that looked like it was used to torture people and he wanted me to be fucking quiet. Be fucking for real. I needed answers, and I needed them now.

My ears perked again hearing shoes clack against the floor outside the door. Seconds later, the door opened, and my eyes landed on a dark figure. It stood there in the doorway not making a peep. The hairs on the back of my neck came to a standstill. Whoever it was, they were looking at me. I sensed it in my soul.

One of his feet stepped into the door, and my heart skipped beats in my chest. His frame came into view, and my eyes danced over his body. Standing before me was one of the sexiest men walking this earth in a custom black suit with chains dangling around his neck. Had we met under different circumstances, I would have sworn he was one of God's angels. This man was tall and lean like a tree. Both of his hands rested in his pockets. His face... stone as his dark eyes went from Mama to me, Coco, and then Daddy.

His walnut-complexioned face was flawless. Almost too impeccable for a man. His plump lips parted, and he asked,

"This isn't all of 'em. Where's Dash and Wick?" He turned and faced the three men that stood behind him.

"I—I don't know. We searched—" Before he could finish his sentence the guy had his hand wrapped firmly around his throat. His face turned purple, and I knew all the air had left his lungs.

"I need Dash and Wick," he said through clenched teeth. "You had strict instructions to bring their asses to me." I wasn't certain why they were looking for my younger brother and his best friend, but I should have known that was the reason why all of us were kneeling before them. Dash couldn't stay out of trouble to save his life. Had Ma not babied him the way she had, maybe he would have turned out more respectful.

Dash was always in some shit. I couldn't count on my hands how many times he fucked up and Daddy had to cover it up. If anyone knew what Daddy did behind closed doors for Dash, he would have been out of office by now.

More feet approached our direction from outside the door. This older guy stepped into the room. He was handsome as hell just like the other man before us. This one had a salt and pepper curly taper and goatee. His white button down had the top buttons undone and his chest hair peeked out. Another younger gentleman stepped in behind him with his hands shoved in his pockets. He was fine, but not as fine as the first guy that entered.

The older gentleman gazed in the first guy's direction and he immediately released his man. That alone told me who was really in charge here.

"They don't know where Dash is," he told him and stepped to his side.

"Can you tell me why we're here?" Daddy finally spoke up.

A wooden chair was placed behind the man in charge and

he took a seat. My eyes darted to the dried-up blood stain on the floor just inches away from my leg. *Yeah, we weren't making it out of here.*

"Your son took something that belongs to me and I want it back," the guy finally spoke.

"Wha-what did he take? Maybe I can get it back for you."

"He and his buddy stole my Aston Martin off my trailer."

"All this for a car?" I blurted, and all three of their eyes cut in my direction. "Daddy, give him the money for the car so we can leave."

"It's not that simple. Hush," he shot back and turned his attention back to the men before us.

"You of all people know how much those cars mean to me," the guy continued, and Daddy nodded.

"I can get you your car back. Just let my family go."

"Now you know I can't do that. Y'all owe us." His eyes shifted to Coco. "And I think I know just how you can pay back your debt." A hot tear rolled down her cheek. "Seeing how my son is supposed to take over the family reins soon, in order for him to do so, he has to be married. I—"

"No! No!" Ma spoke up, and it clicked in my head exactly what he was suggesting. He was absurd.

"Word on the streets is that your daughter is pure."

"Pops..." the first guy interrupted him. He must be the one that was supposed to take over.

Lifting his hand, he silenced him and continued, "In exchange for your lives, your daughter is to marry my son."

"Harvey, you can't let them do this." Ma's hand covered his on his thigh. Her gaze was clouded with tears. "There has to be another way."

"Fine," escaped Daddy's lips, and Coco gasped. He was really about to hand his daughter over on a silver platter to these monsters.

"I volunteer!" I told them, not wanting them to force that shit onto Coco. She didn't deserve that. Not her of all people. No way I was gon' sit here and allow them to pawn her off on a stranger like that. She had so much potential and life to live. If someone had to save the entire family, it was gon' be me.

The second guy's head tilted to the side and his lips parted, "You're a virgin?"

"What are you trying to say? I don't look like I'm pure?"

"Honey, I've seen your name in the headlines more than anyone."

"That's a lie," I protested, and he frowned. No one has been in the headlines more than Dash. That was a fact. "I might like to party, but that doesn't mean I'm not pure." Coco and I made a pact when we were twelve that we'd save ourselves for marriage. Both of us were still virgins. I hadn't come across anyone that was worthy enough for me to break my pact with my sister. All the men weren't shit, especially Wick's ass. Every time I turned around, he was sniffing up my ass and any other female he could get close to.

"She's pure?" He eyeballed my parents, and they both shrugged. I didn't open up to them about my sexual life so they wouldn't know if I was pure or not.

"She is," Coco answered, and our gazes synced. "But you don't have to do this for me, Honey. I can do it."

"I volunteer. They aren't about to rip you away from your life. I'll do it. I'm the oldest. I should do it." Besides, I had the stomach for it. Coco, on the other hand, was gon' be miserable as hell had she married him. He wasn't even her type. My eyes danced over his frame. He looked rude as fuck and arrogant. That nigga wasn't gon' do nothing but hurt her feelings, then they really were gon' have to bury all of our asses.

"Great. You'll be wedded in the spring."

The first guy's jaw muscles stiffened. He shoved his hands in his pockets and marched out of there.

"So does that mean we're free to go?" Daddy questioned him.

"You can go, but if I were you, I'd get a handle on that damn Dash. He steps out of line again, I'm gon' fucking destroy you." Lifting to his feet, he said, "Don't fucking forget that my family is the reason why you're in office. I'll fucking destroy you, Governor Harvey," then exited the room with some of his men following him.

CHAPTER TWO
LAWRENCE "LAW" BLANCO

Marriage... some bullshit I was being forced into. With me being the oldest, I was always supposed to be the successor of the Blanco Mafia. Pops mentioned to me 'bout me having to be married and shit, but when I spoke to him 'bout not wanting a bride, I thought he'd drop the shit. Being married never worked out for him, so I knew damn well the shit wasn't for me. I was cool being single and able to slide up in whatever I wanted when I wanted without the pressure of the headache with a relationship.

"Law, babe, right there," Shayla moaned as my dick tapped her guts. My hand wrapped firmly 'round her throat and I glared down into her beautiful face. Sweat beads dripped from my forehead down to her face like raindrops. With every thrust, Shayla's breasts bounced.

With all the heavy shit on my mind, I had to get the fuck out of that house and relieve some stress. In just a couple months, I was 'bout to be married to some bitch I didn't even know. What threw me for a loop was the fact that Pops agreed that it was Honey I wedded instead of Coco. At least Coco was a lil more conservative than Honey. All that bitch ever did was party and post provocative pictures on social media. Ain't no way she was a fucking virgin. Somebody was smashing that pussy and I was gon' find out exactly who.

Shayla clawed at my hand. Her face began to turn blue. My nut was close; I could feel it building up. A couple more pumps, and I emptied my seeds into my condom and released my death grip on her.

"Got—" She coughed. "Got damn. You trying to kill me?" She gently stroked her neck as she glowered at me. Eyes red as if she'd smoke a pound of kush.

Without uttering a single word, I removed myself from on top of her and crawled out of bed. I padded to her bathroom, pulled the condom off, and dropped it into the toilet. Grabbing a rag, I cleaned myself up and went back into the bedroom. Shayla lay there in bed gawking at me. She smacked her lips when I picked my briefs up from the floor and stepped into 'em.

"Must you always fuck me and leave?" She was just complaining 'bout me almost killing her and now she wanted me to stay the night. Bitches.

"You already know wassup, Shayla."

Sitting up in bed, she eyed me as I gathered the rest of my clothes and got back dressed. "I know, but for once can you just spend the night with me?"

"No," I simply replied and swiped my phone off the nightstand. I didn't spend the night with anyone. That was too intimate for me. As long as I kept 'em at arm's length, I wasn't able to catch feelings.

"Law," she whined and folded her arms over her chest. "Please, I'm begging you. I'm tired of feeling like a jump off. I want to be held. I want to fall asleep in your arms. I need affection."

Facing her, I replied, "I'on do affection. If that's what you fucking want, go find it elsewhere," and exited her bedroom, heading for the front door.

My phone chimed soon as my feet touched the porch.

Streets: *The car turned up at the dealership.*

Me: *On my way.*

Fredrick, my driver, got out the blacked-out Escalade and opened the back door for me. "Take me to Foreign Blanco," I instructed him and climbed into the truck. Nodding, he shut the door and rounded to the driver's side.

Foreign Blanco was our exotic whips dealership. We supplied the south with foreign cars. If it was something you wanted, better believe we can get our hands on it for the right price. Foreign Blanco was family operated, but I was the chief operating officer. Pops planned on stepping down and making me CEO once I took the reins.

The truck came to a halt, pulling me from my thoughts. I peered out the window at the glass building. The entire building wasn't made up of fiberglass, just the front, but the shit was beautiful. From where I sat, I saw the yellow Lamborghini with zero miles on it sitting in the show room. We didn't leave any cars out on the lot 'cause fucking with people here, they'd run their stupid asses on it and take 'em. They be quick to sign their own death certificates.

Streets stood in the parking lot with TP in front of the Aston Martin that was stolen hours prior. Fredrick rounded to my door and opened it for me. I climbed out and strolled over to where Streets and TP stood. The trunk was open, prompting me to ask, "Is it still in there?"

Streets faced me with his hands in his pockets and replied, "Yeah. Looks like all is accounted for."

I stepped to the trunk and my eyes focused on the kilos that rested in there. Of course, Foreign Blanco was a front for our drug empire. We made excellent money off the cars, but we brought in a whole lot more cash flow with the drugs. Not many people knew what we were doing when we got cars delivered. Shit, not even the drivers. They were paid hefty to do their jobs: get our cars here safely and gone 'bout their business.

Wick and Dash didn't know what was inside that car. They were too focused on stealing it so they could try their odds at selling it. Wick and Dash had been a problem in the streets for some time now, doing all sorts of petty crimes. I've spoken to Governor Hurts several times 'bout him getting his son in order. At the rate he was going, he was gon' turn up dead somewhere and not at my hands either.

"What 'bout Wick and Dash?"

"They were long gone by the time we got here," Streets answered. My teeth clenched.

"Take that shit into the warehouse and unload it," I ordered TP, and he nodded. Closing the trunk, he hopped into the driver's seat and pulled off.

"You did anymore thought 'bout that wedding shit?" Streets asked me as we neared our rides.

My eyes cut in his direction. "I'm gon' play along for now, but there's a loophole. I'm gon' figure out exactly what it is, but I ain't marrying that bitch," I told him and climbed into the truck.

CHAPTER THREE
DASH HURTS

"Where's the car?" Wick asked me as I approached his car that was parked on the side of the road in front of J Quick Car Wash. He shut his driver's door behind him and gave me his undivided attention.

"Did you know that shit was filled with drugs?"

"Yeah, duh. Why else I told you to help me get it?"

I shoved him hard in the chest, and he stumbled back against the car. "And you had me driving 'round in that shit!"

"What's the big fucking deal? What you did with the car?"

"I gave that shit back. You're not 'bout to get me killed over that shit."

"Are you crazy!" He shoved me and I slipped on the gravel.

"You the crazy one!" Gaining my composure, I pushed his ass right back. "I could have got caught with that shit! Do you not know what would have happened if I got caught with that shit!"

"And if you did, you would have got right off like you always do." The corner of his mouth quirked, and I wanted to slap that smug ass expression off his face.

"Shit not that fucking easy."

"How?" His head cocked. "You're the governor's son. You can get away with murder if you really wanted to."

"This the exact reason why nobody wants me fucking with you." Spinning on my heels, I trekked off, but he caught me by the forearm. Wick's nostrils flared.

"You really gave the fucking car back?"

Yanking away from his incompetent ass, I replied, "Since when have you ever known me to lie?"

"Are you fucking stupid?" He brushed his shoulder-length locs back out his face. "That could have been a great payday for us. Why you gotta be so immature?"

"If not wanting to get my family killed 'cause of my fuck up makes me immature, then I'll be that. The next time you come up with some stupid ass plan that can get both of us killed, leave me the fuck out of it," I told him and climbed back into my Charger.

I pulled into the gate of the governor's house and parked. It was going on three in the morning and I was surprised nobody had been searching for me. Pops didn't place any men on me anymore 'cause nobody really wanted to deal with me. They all told him I was too much trouble. Lil did they know, I caused hell for 'em 'cause I didn't want 'em up my ass twenty-four-seven like that.

Getting out my car, I climbed the couple steps to the front door and one of the two men guarding it pulled the door open. I climbed the staircase to the second floor and crept past my parents' suite. The door creaked open behind me, and I heard, "Dash, get your ass over here right now."

My body tensed. With how late it was, I was expecting

Pops to still be sleeping. "I'm tired. Can whatever it is wait 'til in the morning?" I tossed over my shoulder.

"If you don't get yo' ass over here, it's gon' take every guard in this house to pull me off yo' ass."

Sighing, I spun on my heels and faced him. He stood there in his blue Versace robe tied tightly 'round his waist and his matching slippers. Glancing over his shoulder, he pulled the door up behind him and took a step closer to me. I closed the gap between us. His hands firmly clutched my shirt and my body slammed into the wall next to their bedroom. "What the fuck were you thinking? Huh!"

Sweat beads formed on my forehead. He couldn't know what I'd been out doing. Could he? Nah. I was gon' play stupid with him like I didn't know what he was talking 'bout. "What are you talking 'bout?"

His jaw muscles tightened, and a vein pulsated in the center of his forehead. It was the exact vein that threatened to pop every time he was pissed with me. "You could have gotten all of us killed. What the fuck were you thinking going out and stealing that car from the Blancos?"

"Look, I didn't know it was their car let alone what was in it."

"Why the fuck are you out stealing cars anyway? I'm so tired of cleaning up your fucking shit."

I swallowed the lump in my throat. "So they know I was the one who took it?"

"Duh. And 'cause of your stupid ass decision, you put everyone in danger."

"Is everyone okay?"

"For now they is, but thanks to you, Honey has to marry Law."

My brows furrowed and his grip on me released. I smoothed out the wrinkles in my shirt. His hand swept across his head and he turned, giving me his back. "Why does she have to marry Law?"

Facing me, he replied, "They wanted Coco, but you already know how protective of her she is. To fix your mistake and save the entire family, I had to give up my fucking child."

"I'm sorry. I can fix this. Since I gave the car back, maybe they'll call the wedding off."

"Shit don't work like that, son. The Blancos are very dangerous people. If there's something they want, nothing or no one will stop them."

"What's that supposed to mean?"

"It means that you got one more fuck up and I'm sending your ass to stay with your grandmother." Without uttering another word, he went back into his room and shut the door behind him.

CHAPTER FOUR
COCO HURTS
A COUPLE NIGHTS LATER

"C'mon, Co, it's just for a few hours then you can come back and finish studying," Honey begged me in my ear from behind. Her hands rested firmly on the top of my chair. Here I was sitting in my room minding my business, trying to study for a test that was coming up, and she was begging me to go out to a frat party. If one asked me, she had bigger things on her mind than to be getting wasted at a party. Like how she agreed to marry some stranger. I pleaded with Honey all the way home that night, but she wasn't changing her mind. We went from worrying about planning our birthday party to having to plan a wedding. This was insane.

I cut my eyes at Honey and her champagne-colored ones stared back at me. "I really need to study for this test."

Her lips pursed. "Co, you're the smartest person I know. Knowing you, you probably studied that same shit a million times. Get outta your head. I'm sure it won't hurt if you got out for a bit."

"Fine, but only for a couple hours."

Honey's arms craned around me tightly. "Thank you! Marcia is going to meet us there."

"Of course she is. Let me find me something to wear."

Honey straightened her posture and exited my bedroom. I closed my MacBook and books then lifted from my desk. Trudging to my walk-in closet, I stepped inside and scanned my clothes for something I could toss on. I decided on this white asymmetrical skort, a brown tank top, and my brown plaid coat.

Entering my bathroom from the back of my closet, I turned on the shower and stripped out my clothes. The best thing about staying in the governor's house was my beautiful suite and bathroom. I could live in this bathroom for forever. From the gorgeous white and gray marble floors to the garden tub and the walk-in shower. This bathroom was every girl's dream.

For the last three years, Daddy had been governor. Our lives changed before my eyes. One moment, he was coming home with the brilliant idea to run, then the next we were ripped from our lives. People were always in our business. Once they saw he had daughters, my social medias blew up. I barely posted anything. I hated the attention, but Honey, on the other hand, thrived off it. She was certainly the yin to my yang.

After my shower, I got dressed and went to find Honey. Her outfit was cute as fuck. She rocked this red and white plaid coat and a white jumpsuit. Her chestnut brown hair was in loose curls flowing over her shoulders.

"You ready?" she asked, puckering her lips and rolling her Fenty gloss on.

"Yeah. Just a couple hours," I reminded her in case she wanted to pretend as if she forgot.

Snickering, she responded, "The truck is waiting for us out front."

We exited her bedroom and went downstairs. The guards at the door opened the double doors for us and we stepped onto the porch. The black Tahoe truck sat there in the circular driveway. Soon as he saw us, the driver jumped from the truck and opened the back door for us.

Daddy had so many men in his security detail that I couldn't even remember most of their names. I knew the regulars by face, but that was about it.

The ride to the party at the Omega Psi Phi house was a silent one for the most part. Honey kept giggling at something on her phone. For the life of me, I couldn't really understand how she was so cheerful when her life was about to change for forever.

The truck halted, bringing me from my thoughts. I looked up and saw that we were parked out front of the Omega house. There were at least ten people standing in line at the door. Honey leaned over me and peeped out at the house. It was a white two-story home. From the outside, it looked like a regular house, but all the shit that went down inside that house would have people amazed. Going to frat parties was Honey's and Marcia's thing. I would have rather stayed home snuggled up with a good book.

"Marcia said she's already inside. Let's go."

I blankly stared at the side of my sister's face and wanted to ask her how the hell she was holding it together so well. Honey was strong as hell. She'd always been. Sometimes I wished I had her strength, but I know God gave us differences and that's what really made us unique.

Climbing out the truck, I followed Honey up to the front door. All eyes rested on us as we climbed the steps, bypassing everyone who had been waiting in line for God only knows how long. I hugged myself and shifted my eyes elsewhere as if I didn't feel theirs burning holes in my flesh.

"Not so fast, ladies." Drek stuck his arm out and stopped Honey from crossing the threshold. "The sign states that you have to take a shot before entering." He nodded toward the paper sign next to his head that was written in red Sharpie. Picking up the bottle of Casamigos off the table, he grabbed some plastic shot cups and poured each of us a shot.

"No thank you," I rejected him and pushed his hand away before the cup could fully reach me. I didn't drink. I was a light weight. That one shot was gon' put me on my ass.

"No shot, no entry."

"C'mon, Drek, can't you just cut her a break?" My eyes darted to Honey who had already tossed back her shot as if it was a sip of water.

"Look, I'on make the rules, I just enforce 'em. No shot, no entry."

"Fine." Snatching the cup from him, I tossed it back and squeezed my eyes shut as the liquid burned my throat like the fire pits of hell.

"Atta girl. Go right ahead. Y'all have fun."

Honey took me by the hand and led me into the house. LED lights lined the ceiling and floorboards, jumping from different colors. There were so many people in the living room that you could barely maneuver it. "Stay close," Honey tossed over her shoulder. "Have you seen Marcia?" she asked some chick that was passing, and she shook her head.

"Did you try calling her?" I questioned.

She pulled me to the side and took her phone out her jacket pocket. The light from the phone illuminated her face as she stood there waiting for Marcia to answer. My eyes drifted around the party. One guy was in the corner of the room with his head down and one hand resting against the wall while the other held a red plastic cup. He hurled and vomited out his insides on the floor. A group of guys were on the opposite side of the living room having a smoking session. They had three blunts in rotation and it was only three of them. Grabbing my mane, I brought it up to my nose and inhaled. It still smelled like fresh strawberries, but by the time I left here, it was gon' reek of weed, vomit, and there's no telling what else. Goosebumps coursed my frame, and I shivered. I was gon' have to scrub myself from head to toe in the shower once I made it back home.

"She's not picking up," Honey finally spoke, snapping me from my thoughts.

"Do you want to walk around and see if you can find her?"

"Yeah!" she yelled over the music and grabbed me by the hand again.

We took the short hallway toward what looked to be the kitchen. Soon as we gained entry, to the right of me was a counter filled with alcohol. "Jackpot," Honey said and went over to the counter. I stood to the side as she grabbed a bottle of Patrón and fixed herself a drink.

"I really don't see how you drink that shit. It's disgusting."

"It's really not. I can mix you up something fruity if you want me to."

"No." I lifted my hand, palm facing her. "I'm going back to study soon, remember?"

"How could I forget?" Latto's "Put It on the Floor Again" beat dropped and Honey's eyes widened like saucers. "Rip me out the plastic, I been actin' brand new. Bitches actin' like they runnin' shit, they really ran through," she sang and took a sip from her drink. She lifted her cup in the air, rested her free hand on her hip and dropped it low, sweeping her small ass across the floor. Honey didn't have a whole lot of ass, but it was slightly bigger than mine. She definitely tossed it around as if it was the ass of all asses. That was another thing I envied about her—she was able to dance her ass off, meanwhile, I didn't have rhythm to save my life. It wasn't like I was gon' get out there and dance if I did. Shaking my ass was just gon' bring unwarranted attention.

"Y'all wanna play beer pong?" a masculine voice asked from behind and I jumped, not knowing that someone else was in the kitchen with us. When I turned around, I saw this handsome, tall ass guy placing cups on the counter. He wore an Omega shirt, letting everyone know he was part of the fraternity.

"Hell yeah," Honey quickly answered and straightened her posture. "I have to find a partner first."

"What 'bout her?" His eyes drifted in my direction and his tongue swept his lips.

"She don't drink," Honey answered for me.

"Don't drink?" He chuckled. "Do you not know where you are and you don't drink?"

"She came out with me. She don't have to drink to have a good time."

"Thank you," I spoke up.

"Let me see where Marcia is." Honey whipped her phone out and went to call Marcia's number 'til we heard her voice coming from another room.

"I'm telling you I can do it!" Marcia yelled.

Honey and I followed the voice. We stepped into the doorway of what looked to be the family room. In the center of the floor was this huge keg with a long clear tube attached to it. Marcia stood next to two large guys. One was so huge he looked like three niggas in one.

"Marcia!" Honey shouted her name, grasping her attention.

"Oh shit! You made it!" Marcia ran over in our direction and embraced both of us.

"I've been calling your phone," Honey told her.

"Didn't hear it."

"You want to be my beer pong partner?"

"Yeah. Give me a minute. I'm 'bout to beat their record." Marcia bounced back over to the keg and the guys gripped her by the ankles and turned her upside down. She grabbed the tube and placed it into her mouth.

"I don't think she's going to be much help after this," I whispered to Honey.

"Marcia! Marcia!" the crowd chanted her name as she chugged that beer.

Moments later, she pulled the tube from her mouth and yelled, "Done!" Everyone began to go crazy. They planted Marcia back on her feet and she jumped up and down. "I told you! Pay up!" She shoved her hands in their direction, palms facing the ceiling and wiggled her fingers. One of the guys slapped five hundred-dollar bills down in her hand.

I never fully understood why Marcia drank as much as she did, or how she stomached that much liquor for that matter. There was this thing with her father never being present in her life and her mama being an alcoholic. Maybe it was genetics. Whatever it was, she was determined to not end up like her mama—the neighborhood drunk. That's how she ended up at Alabama State with us. Clinical doctorate in physical therapy was her degree.

Marcia stumbled in our direction and Honey caught her by the hip, pulling her into her frame. Despite all the shit she'd been through, Marcia was gorgeous as hell. She was one of those popular chicks that every female envied, and every nigga wanted to fuck. Unlike us, Marcia wasn't a virgin. She had long lost her virginity back in our freshman year in high school to a senior that was now serving time in prison for some petty crime.

"Let's play some beer pong."

After a long game of beer pong, Marcia was barely able to stand. She slouched down to the floor against the cabinet. Honey wasn't too far behind her. She stumbled to the floor and rested her head against Marcia's shoulder and giggled. *No way I was gon' be able to get both of them out of here and to the truck by myself.*

"You good?" a masculine voice asked me from behind. It wasn't a strange one. It was the same one from earlier. Though he and his friend had whupped the sleeves off Honey and Marcia in beer pong, he still had his fair share of drinks but didn't seem to be drunk at all. *Maybe he was used to it.*

"You think you can help me get them out to the truck?" Peeking over the island, he saw Honey and Marcia sitting there.

"Yeah, I can help you. Which one I need to grab?"

He rounded the island and I pointed at Marcia, who was already slobbering from the corner of her mouth. Grabbing Honey by the wrists, I pulled her up from the floor and draped her arm around my neck. He scooped Marcia up bridal style and carried her out the door behind me. Soon as the driver saw us, he jumped from the truck and opened the back door. Marcia was gently placed inside then I helped Honey in. Turning to face the guy who helped me, I said, "Thanks."

"No problem. Maybe I'll see you 'round school."

My face turned red as tomato paste. "Maybe." I hopped into the truck and the driver shut the door behind me.

"Where to?" he asked when he got back into the driver's seat.

My stomach grumbled so I asked, "Can you stop by Waffle House along the way home?"

Nodding, he pulled away from the curb. Honey rested her head in my lap while Marcia lay stretched out across from us on the other seats.

"I don't want to get married," Honey said, catching me off guard.

My fingertips gently stroked her hair back out her face and I responded, "Then don't do it."

"It's not that easy, Co. I'm not about to let you ruin your life like that."

"So you'd rather ruin yours?"

"Exactly." She nested her face against my thighs, and I knew it wasn't gon' be long before she fell asleep.

By the time we made it to Waffle House both Honey and Marcia were sound asleep. I eased my body from underneath Honey's head and climbed out the truck.

"I'm just going to order my food and I'll be right back out," I told the driver, and he nodded.

I entered the building, and it was pretty dead in there. Aside from the staff there was one couple and some older guy sitting in the booths. I eased onto one of the barstools and a waitress immediately stepped in front of me.

"What can I get you tonight?"

"I think I want the all-star with bacon, blueberry waffle, and hash brown. Scramble my eggs with cheese and on my hash I want ham bits and cheese," I told her without even having to look at the menu. Waffle House was one of my favorite places to eat. I knew the menu like the back of my hand.

"Coming right up." Turning around, she called out my order just as I heard the door open behind me. The scent of expensive cologne circulated my head as a warm body occupied the stool alongside me.

"You're out late," escaped a pair of lips. When I turned and saw who was sitting next to me, my heart dropped to my lap.

The hairs on my arms lifted as I gazed at the handsome

specimen beside me. Handsome wasn't the word to describe him. God took his time molding this man.

He sat there in this black button up. Two chains nestled around his neck. A tiny gold hoop rested in his ear. My eyes roamed from the side of his caramel face, down his biceps to the Cartier watch glistening on his wrist.

I swallowed hard the lump that formed in my throat. "It's-it's you." His dark eyes bored into mine. "Dash gave the car back. Why don't you ask them to relieve my sister of that silly agreement?"

"I don't interfere with my pops' and brother's affairs. If she agreed to it, the only way she gon' get out that contract is if she ends up at the morgue or him." My body tensed at his response.

"So it's really no way she can get out of it?"

"No," he simply replied and picked up the menu.

"Your food's ready, mama," the waitress made known, grasping my attention. Keeping my eyes trained on him, I pulled my card out and handed it to her.

"Thank you," I told her when she handed me back my card and receipt. Taking one final glimpse of him, I got up from the stool and excited the building. My sister was really about to marry a stranger all just to save me, and I wasn't sure how to feel about it.

CHAPTER FIVE
KOFI "STREETS" BLANCO
A COUPLE DAYS LATER

Leaves and sticks crunched underneath my feet with every step I took. The chilly air nipped at my face, threatening me to pull my coat tighter. This was the coldest it had been all year, which was crazy considering spring was vastly approaching.

My strides halted in front of the huge angel statue that was connected to the tombstone. *Zara Blanco. Beloved daughter and mother.* I removed the dead roses from the flower holder and placed the purple lilies in there that I just purchased prior to coming here. They were her favorite and I always made it my mission to grab 'em for her whenever I came to visit, which was often.

My fingertips grazed the top of the tombstone. "How you holding up?" I asked Ma. My breath formed in front of my face. "I know Law hasn't come and seen you in a while, but he's 'bout to get married." I chuckled 'cause I could hear her now. Law and the word marriage didn't even go hand in hand. "It's some arrangement that Pops set up. You know he wouldn't be getting married any other way, especially after what happened to you. That boy swore off marriage for good. Anyways, I just came to check in on you and make sure you were straight."

Kissing my middle and index finger, I pressed 'em against the tombstone and shoved my hands into my coat pockets. "I love you. I'll catch you later."

I trotted back to the truck, passing some older woman who was standing in front of another tombstone. I'd noticed her there from time to time but wasn't quite sure who she'd been visiting. Each time I saw her, she stood there not uttering a word but bawled her eyes out. John jumped from the truck and opened the back door for me.

"Where you heading?" he questioned.

"Dalriada," I simply answered and slid into the back seat.

It took us a while to make it to Dalriada. Once we got there, I instructed John to stop by this salon that was in the shopping center. Pulling up to the door, he opened the truck door for me, and I stepped down out. "I'll be right back," I told him and lifted my foot to walk, but it got pulled back to the ground. Lifting my foot again, I saw there was a piece of pink chewing gum stuck between the bottom of my red bottom and the ground.

Scrubbing my foot against the ground, I proceeded toward the doors of Trina's Cuts. The door chimed when I entered, and all chatter stopped soon as the stylists' eyes landed on me. It was still quite early so there weren't any customers in the building yet. My eyes bounced 'round the tiny establishment. Everything was pink as if Pepto Bismol exploded inside here. The shit was tacky as fuck. The rug was one color pink and the sinks and chairs were other color pinks. This shit was nothing but an eye sore and I couldn't wait to get the fuck out of here.

"Where's Trina?" I asked no one in particular.

"She's in her office. You want me to go get her?"

"Nah." I strolled to the back of the salon where Trina's

office was located. Not even bothering to knock on the door, I barged straight in and stopped soon as my eyes landed on her bent over her desk with some bald-headed nigga plowing her from behind. Both of their heads snapped in my direction.

"Got damn, nigga, you can't knock?" The nigga pulled himself out of Trina and stuffed his dick back into his pants. He lifted his foot to march in my direction, but Trina jumped in front of him and pushed him back.

"It's fine. It's fine," she said and pulled her dress down over her fat ass. "I don't have all the money yet," Trina went to explain. "Just give me a couple weeks and I'll have it." My eyes roamed her from head to toe. This bitch had a fresh wig on her head and her nails were recently done. Instead of holding on to the money she was supposed to pay us, she was out here blowing the shit on irrelevant ass shit.

"Trina, you said that same bullshit two weeks ago. I gave you two weeks already, I can't extend you any more time. I need those ends before Law be the one standing here the next time, and we both know you don't want that. Had it been Law, this place would have already been burned to the ground by now. You knew the terms to the agreement when you signed on that line. Get me my fucking money. You got two days," I told her and exited the office.

I sauntered out the door, ignoring the whispers as I passed. "Go make sure she gets the fucking memo," I told John and stopped by the truck with my back facing the entrance. Nodding, he passed me and went into the salon. Seconds later, I heard screams and all sorts of shit breaking behind me. I pulled a pre-rolled blunt from my pocket and tucked it securely between my lips, lighting the tip of it. When I turned 'round, John exited the door and opened the back door for me.

'Bout two months ago, Trina came to my family's loan company in need of a loan. Business had been slow, and she needed help paying the bills that month and to stay afloat for a while. She'd been making her payments faithful 'til a few weeks ago. I sent one of the men to come collect and she ain't have the money. Claimed shit was slowing down again, but that wasn't my problem. She signed a promise to pay, and I wanted my fucking bread.

I never did pickups unless we were having an issue. If that problem couldn't get resolved by me, Law would step in. I was the more lenient brother. I tried to give you a chance. Law, on the other hand, he'd shoot and ask questions later. Everyone knew that if Law showed his face, there was hell to pay.

John took me by Blanco's Loans to make certain that everything was straight before I headed to the dealership. That was one of the many places we owned in Montgomery. Sure, we made money the illegal way, but we made certain that we had several legitimate businesses as well to cover our asses. Some might think it was crazy that we were still out here in these streets when we had more money than we could count. We could have been retired by now. That's the plan once we got old enough and had a heir to secure the throne. 'Til then, we were out here ruling the hell out of these Montgomery streets.

It's funny 'cause I got my nickname from my mama. She started calling me Streets 'cause she couldn't get me to stay out of 'em to save her life when I was growing up. I hated being confined by walls. I loved fresh air. Law used to joke 'bout me going crazy if I were ever forced to do a stint in prison. I see no lies told.

John pulled into the handicap space of Blanco's Loans and opened the door for me. I climbed out and saw a Charger parked next to us. The tint on the car was so fucking dark that I was certain the cops had a field day pulling it over every chance they got.

John opened the door for me and I entered the building.

There were a couple people standing in line but the one who stood out to me the most was the nigga sitting in one of the chairs by the window. He lifted to his feet and brushed his hand 'cross his sandy brown waves. He stepped his freckle-faced ass in my path and my hand craned behind my back and gripped my strap in my waistline.

"Don't!" he all but yelled with his hand in the air. "I come in peace. I just wanted to speak to you."

"You got a lot of fucking nerves showing your got damn face in here after what the fuck you did."

"I swear I didn't know what was in that trunk. After I found out, I returned the car. That was all Wick's idea."

"You got one foot in the grave. I suggest you find better friends."

Releasing the handle of my gun, I straightened my coat.

"Can I talk to you 'bout Honey?"

My eyes darted over the top of his head, and I replied, "You're barking up the wrong tree."

"Can you at least talk to 'em? Tell 'em I'll pay off my debt, just leave her out of it."

My jaw muscles tightened. "Just like I told your sister, I don't interfere with other people's affairs."

"Wait, you talked to Honey?"

My gaze met his and I replied, "No."

"Oooh, Coco. I should have known she was gon' try and fix things."

"I can't help you. Now get the fuck out of here before I have John here toss you out on your ass."

His eyes peeked 'round me to John who was standing tall behind me. John was an ex-marine. That nigga was big and tall. One thing for sure 'bout him, when he shoots, he never misses. That was the exact reason why I kept him at my side.

Clenching his teeth, he shoved his hands into his pockets

and strolled out of there. Had he kept his fucking hands to himself, his sister wouldn't be in the predicament she was in. He couldn't fault anyone but himself.

"Hey, Streets, there's an important phone call for you. Want me to transfer it to your office?" Charlene asked through the bulletproof glass.

Nodding, I treaded to my office.

CHAPTER SIX
HONEY

"Oh my God, my head is throbbing." I closed my eyes and gently massaged my temples.

"That's what you get for staying out all night last night and knew you had to go to class this morning. Honestly, I don't know how you and Marcia do it."

"Co, will you just shut up. You're making it worse."

"Here. You should feel better in no time."

Peeking out my right eye, I saw a Goody Powder in Coco's hand. Snatching it from her, I ripped it open and poured the contents on my tongue. My face scrunched as I swallowed it. Grabbing my pink Starbucks cup, I chased it with fruit juice.

"I'm so ready to go in the house and lay down," I told Co as the truck turned into the driveway.

"So much for you laying down," Coco said, grasping my attention. I looked out the window and saw Ma and Daddy standing on the porch. He held an envelope in his hand. The last time I saw them standing outside like that, waiting for us to arrive home from school, I was failing math class.

"Fuck," I said, mumbling underneath my breath.

The truck stopped and I didn't even wait for the driver to come around and open the door for me. I jumped out and stopped short in front of them. Folding my arms over my chest, I said, "What now?"

"We need to speak with you," Daddy said and went back into the house with Ma right on his heels. They stepped into the conference room that was mere inches away from the front door. "Have a seat." He gestured to the long, mahogany rectangular table. Pulling out one of the chairs, I sat down and braced myself for whatever was about to come out of his mouth.

"Your contract came over this morning."

"Contract?" My brows furrowed.

"Yes. Contract," he said and took a seat at the table across from me with my mama opposite of him. "When you agreed to marry Law, they drew up a contract for you to sign so that you can't back out of it."

"Are you fucking serious?"

Opening the envelope, he slid it over in front of me. "I've looked over it already. It's pretty solid. You have to marry in the spring and within a year, you must produce an heir."

"What!" My eyes expanded and mouth dropped to the table. "I'm still in school. I'm not trying to have any kids right now. Have they lost their mind! Nope. I'm not doing it." Slamming my hands down against the table, I pushed up from my seat. "You can send that right on back to them and tell them I'm not doing it. They can shove it up their ass far as I care."

Daddy caught me by the wrist before I was able to exit the room. "You don't really have much of a choice. The Blancos believe that word is bond. You agreed to take Coco's place and that's what you must do. If you don't, you can put all of us in danger."

I swallowed hard the lump that formed in my throat and

shut my eyes. After a couple deep breaths, I went back over to my seat. "Give me a pen," I told them. If me signing away my life was gon' save everyone else's then I had no other choice.

"Once you sign this paper, you must pack up everything you'll need and go over to the mansion immediately," Daddy instructed me.

The ball of the pen sat on the line as my mind ran a million miles a minute. With the stroke of a pen, my life was about to change forever. The day I had been dreading finally presented itself and there was no way I was getting out of this.

"Honey?" my mama softly spoke, and our gazes meet. "Down the line, you might fall in love with him. You never know."

Warm tears strolled my cheeks. "Ma, this isn't a fairytale. This is real life and I doubt very seriously that I'll fall in love with a man like him."

"Look on the bright side. It does say that you can get out of your contract if something was to ever happen to Law and he died before the wedding."

"Harvey!" Ma shrieked.

His head snapped in her direction. "What? I was just letting our daughter know exactly what she was signing. If God is on our side, Law will die before the wedding date."

I scribbled my name on the line and shoved the papers over to Daddy. They flew over the desk, all over him and the floor. "I guess I'll go pack my things," I said and lifted to my feet then stormed out of there.

Marching upstairs to my bedroom, I stopped in the doorway and found Coco sitting on my bed.

"What happened?" hurriedly escaped her lips, and she bolted to her feet.

"I have to pack. They want me to move into his house today. I had to sign a contract stating that I'll produce them a baby within the first year of marriage." After those words seeped from my lips, I stumbled over to my bed and eased down on the edge. Warm tears trickled my cheeks. "They're ripping me away from my life. I'm not ready for a kid right now."

"I'm so sorry, Honey. I tried to tell you to just let me gon' and do it. You're so stubborn." Coco sat down alongside me and draped her arm around me. My head rested against her.

"Can you at least help me pack?" Though they were tossing things at me that I wasn't prepared for, I still was gon' bite the bullet and take Coco's place.

"Whatever you need."

Drying my eyes with the collar of my shirt, I rose to my feet and proceeded to pack whatever I thought I might need to take. For the next couple of hours, Coco helped me pack my things. I had four suitcases filled with my items. That was nowhere near everything I acquired while we lived here. There was no point in taking everything because I figured they'd give me more things once I got settled.

A guy dressed in a finely tailored black suit stepped into my doorway with my daddy directly behind him. "Your ride has come to take you to your new home," he said so proudly.

Turning to Coco, I grabbed her and pulled her into an embrace. Her tears dampened my shoulder as we hugged. We were really standing here saying goodbye as if we'd never see each other again.

"I love you," she said as we peeled apart.

"I love you too."

I marched out of the bedroom while Daddy and the other guy grabbed my things. Ma was waiting for me downstairs by the front door. "Where's Dash?" I asked, noticing that I hadn't really seen him around the last couple of days, especially since all of this was his fault in the first place.

"I don't know. I haven't seen him," she answered and grabbed me by the hands. Her eyes bordered with tears. "I'm really sorry that you have to go through this. This isn't something I've ever wanted for you."

"It's okay, Ma. Long as everyone else is safe. I'll do anything for y'all," I replied, meaning every word.

Daddy and the guy brushed past me outside with my luggage. Ma pecked me gently on the corner of the mouth and released my hands. "Call me any time that you need me. I don't care what time it is. You know I'll come running." She brushed her tears with her fingertips.

Nodding, I stepped out onto the porch, finding a blacked-out Escalade parked out front. Another guy grabbed my suitcases from Daddy and placed them into the trunk. One of them opened the back door for me as I approached the truck.

"I'll be by to check on you," Daddy said.

"Whatever," rolled off my tongue. True enough, it wasn't right to be treating him the way I was since it wasn't really his fault I was in this predicament, but I was angry. Mad that the life I once knew was gon' be no more. As I climbed into the truck, I pulled out my phone and shot Dash a text. *You owe me your fucking life.* The door shut behind me and soon, the truck pulled off.

Thirty-five minutes later, we were pulling up to the gate of a mansion. Two large lion statues rested on either side of it at the top. The gate buzzed and the doors opened. I gasped as I took in the house in front of me. This certainly wasn't the one we were at the day we got kidnapped. That one was huge as well, but this one... it really took the cake. The house was just about as big as the governor's mansion. And I was about to live here.

The landscape was immaculate. The bushes were trimmed to perfection. The grass was freshly cut and green as if someone painted it. The house was a beige brick with what looked like a million windows.

The driver pulled around the small, circular patch of grass that housed a water fountain and stopped at the front door. The huge mahogany double doors opened, and this woman stepped out onto the porch with this guy dressed in a gray suit behind her. The woman was short, maybe five four, with shoulder-length salt and pepper hair. Her eyes were emerald. She was tiny and looked fragile to the touch.

The truck stopped and the back door was opened for me. I eased out, and the woman clasped her hands together, pressing them against her lips. "Oh my God, look at you. You're so beautiful," she cooed, inching toward me. "Nigel, help with her things," she instructed the guy on the porch with her. Without uttering a word, he stepped away and went over to the truck. Sticking her small, wrinkled hands out in my direction, she grabbed me by mine and her eyes twinkled as she scrutinized me. "I told them that I wanted to be here to meet my new grandbaby. Law did good with you. You're so gorgeous."

My cheeks burned. This woman seemed so sweet. How the hell could she be attached to such monsters like that?

"I'm Ada, by the way. You and Law will make some beautiful great-grandbabies." I cringed at the thought of it. "Nigel is going to show you where you'll be sleeping. I left my phone number on your nightstand in case you ever need me. I have an appointment to go to, but we can grab lunch later in the week so we can get to know each other." I nodded. There was no way I was gon' skip out on lunch with her. She was probably the sanest person I'd encounter in this marriage. If I was gon' be in this hell hole, I was gon' need a friend.

"Let me show you to your bedroom," Nigel said when he entered the house. I stepped over the threshold behind him and was in awe. The foyer had a huge gold chandelier hanging from the ceiling. I followed him up the staircase and over the catwalk down a hallway.

"Your room is right this way," he said and pushed a door in.

My eyes wandered the gorgeous space. It was about the same size of my old bedroom. The bed was gold and white with a huge, tufted headboard. A gold and diamond chandelier hung from the ceiling just above the bed. There were two tufted chairs at the foot of the bed with a fluffy white throw tossed over one.

Nigel set my suitcases on the floor and said, "I'll go get the rest of your bags. Let me know if you need anything."

"Hey, so Law doesn't sleep in here?"

"No. He stays on the opposite side of the house. This is where you'll stay during your marriage. You are forbidden from entering his bedroom."

"Are you serious?" My right brow arched. I wasn't complaining, but I just wanted to make sure he wasn't playing a joke on me. Separate bedrooms weren't an issue for me. The less time I spent with him the better.

"Please, just stay out of his bedroom," was the only thing he said before exiting mine.

CHAPTER SEVEN
LAW
THE FOLLOWING MORNING

The knock at my bedroom door grasped my attention. "Come in," I poked my head out and said from the walk-in closet.

"Mr. TP is waiting for you downstairs," Nigel said from the bedroom.

Grabbing my Armani suit jacket, I exited the closet. "Have him meet me in my office. I'll be there shortly." Nodding, he left the room and shut the door behind him.

The day before, Honey was brought over to the house. I came in late, so I wasn't able to see her. This was gon' be the first time being in her presence since the night they were brought to Pops' house. For days, I had been trying to figure out a way to get out of this shit. Pops told me that if I didn't want to marry Honey, then I could just hand the reins over to Streets, and he could do it. Pops knew I wasn't 'bout to willingly do that bullshit. Ever since I was ten, I'd been groomed to take over the family business. It was my birth right. If me marrying Honey was the only way, then I was gon' marry her ass. He said that we had to be bond legally, he didn't say anything 'bout me having to deal with her. That's the exact reason why I put her ass on the opposite side of the house.

Swiping my pistol off the nightstand, I slipped it into my waistline and exited the bedroom. My office was on the first floor back by the family room. It took me no time to get there. TP was sitting in one of the chairs in front of my mahogany desk. Shutting the door behind me, I rounded the desk and took my seat.

"What you got for me?" I questioned him and relaxed back in my seat.

TP pursed his lips and brushed his hand across his temp fade. "Nothing."

Leaning forward, I interlocked my fingers, resting my hands on the desk and asked, "What the fuck you mean nothing?"

Shrugging, he responded. "Nothing. Absolutely nothing came back on her. She's only had two boyfriends in her life and neither one of 'em ever had sex with her. She's a virgin. She may not be as clean as you hoped, but she's a virgin."

"Damn," escaped my lips and I rested back against my chair. "So she was telling the truth. I'm gon' entertain this bullshit for now. I'll be at the dealership after breakfast," I told him and got up from the desk.

TP nodded, rose to his feet, and exited the office. My eyes drifted to the box of cigars on my desk. It was tempting, but it was a lil too early to indulge in those activities.

"Breakfast is ready, sir," Nigel said from the doorway.

Rounding my desk, I followed him toward the dining room where I found Honey sitting at the gold table. That was raw beauty. Her hair was pulled back in a ponytail at the nape of her neck. Her flawless gold skin beamed as if a ray of sun shone directly on her. Honey's gaze meshed with mine once she noticed me standing there, and I broke it.

Taking my seat at the head of the table where my plate was already prepared, I grabbed my glass of orange juice to quench my thirst before I started the conversation that I knew was gon' need to be had.

"I'm glad I caught you this morning. I'm guessing Nigel showed you around the house." She nodded and took a bite from her toast. I ground my teeth at the sound of her crunching her food. Everything 'bout her annoyed the fuck out of me. "I wanted to go over some things with you since we'll be sharing the same living space. Under no circumstances are you to ever enter my bedroom. On the outside, we can be husband and wife to a certain extent, but on the inside, we keep our distance. I don't care what you do with yourself long as you don't bring any trouble to my doorstep. Don't bring over unwanted guests. Keep them at a minimum. Preferably family."

"What about my best friend?"

"Is she trouble?"

Her brows snapped together, and she replied, "No."

"I guess she can come. I only agreed to this shit 'cause I need you. Don't expect no affection from me. Don't come to me with your problems. I'm not your friend nor am I your therapist. We are only bound to each other 'til death. I don't do PDA, so don't expect any from me."

"So basically we're just going to be living together. You have your own life and I have mine?"

"Correct."

"You're controlling as fuck. No wonder why they had to force someone to marry you. No woman in her right mind would want you. Oh, and let's not forget you're a monster." She crunched down on her piece of bacon. Honey didn't know shit 'bout me to be judging me in that manner.

"I don't give a damn what you think of me. This monster is

gon' make sure you're damn taken care of, just follow my rules and we won't have any problems," I told her and proceeded to eat my food. The remainder of breakfast, we sat there in silence. Once I was done eating, Nigel cleared the table and I told him, "Make sure that Honey gets her things," and lifted to my feet.

Nodding, Nigel exited the dining room and came back moments later with a set of keys and a black Amex card on a silver platter. He took it over to Honey. Her eyes shot from the platter to me. "Well taken care of," was all I said before slipping my coat on and exiting the room.

"We have a trailer coming in today. It's supposed to have Mr. Will's truck on there. He's been calling and getting on my fucking nerves 'bout that truck ever since he ordered it."

"Did you tell him how long it was gon' take to get here?" TP questioned me as he sat across from me at my desk.

"Yeah, but that didn't stop him from calling every fucking week to see if it's arrived. I can't wait 'til he gets that shit 'cause I'm two seconds away from going over to his house and placing lead in between his eyes."

TP chuckled but I was serious as a heart attack. Will was getting on my last nerves. This was gon' be the last time he placed an order with me. I don't give a damn how much money he offered; it wasn't worth the headache.

"Excuse me, Law?" Maya, my receptionist, said from the doorway. "There's a young woman out here in the lobby that's insisting on seeing you."

"What does she want?"

"She didn't really say. Said that she wanted to deal with you and you only."

My eyes cut to TP, and he shrugged. "I'll be there in a second." Maya nodded and slipped away from my doorway.

"Maybe it's one of those bitches you been fucking," TP chortled. I bared my teeth. Anyone I dealt with on a personal level knew not to show up to my place of business in search of me no matter what the fuck they wanted.

"Keep an eye on that shipment and make sure that nigga gets that fucking truck," I instructed him and got up from my seat.

Exiting my office, I went into the lobby and found this woman admiring the Rolls Royce that sat in the showroom. From behind, she was thick in all the right places with knotless braids that went past her fat ass. She wore these black denims and a black trench coat.

"It's beautiful, isn't it?" I asked, and she jumped, facing me. Whoever this woman was, she was gorgeous as hell. Her full lips curved into a smile on her butter pecan face.

"It's just gorgeous. How much does a car like this run for?"

"Over a quarter million."

Her eyes expanded. "Yeah, I can't afford this."

"What's your price range?"

"I think I might need something more of a G Wagon's speed or something. I'm not trying to break the bank."

"One of my other employees could have helped you with that. Why me?"

She took a couple steps toward me, and her subtle scent crept up my nostrils. "I heard you were the best in the business and if I wanted to get treated right, I needed to deal with you." Her tongue swept her lips. Shawty wasn't in here thinking 'bout no fucking car. Dick was written all over her brain.

"Well, if you insist. I have a few G Wagons out back if you want to take a look at 'em."

"Sure." She flashed me a smile.

"Let me grab my coat." I went back into my office and grabbed my coat off the rack. Slipping it on, I went back into the lobby to meet back up with shawty. "After you." I gestured toward the exit and she trotted in that direction.

We went around back to the parking lot that separated the building from the warehouse. I took her over to the few G Wagons that we had in stock.

"This one is gorgeous," she said, referring to the pearl white one with twenty-two-inch forged wheels.

"That one just came in a couple weeks ago." I opened the door for her, and she slipped into the butter seat. Her fingertips grazed the steering wheel.

"Yeah, this is niiiiice."

"You can take it for a test drive if you want. I'll go grab the keys."

"Great."

Pulling my phone from my pocket, I shot Maya a text letting her know I needed the keys for the G Wagon. She met me at the door with 'em and I went back to the truck. Climbing into the passenger seat, I handed shawty the keys. She started the truck and pulled out the parking space.

"What made you get into selling cars?"

"It's a family business." Her eyes cut in my direction when I told her that.

"Is that so?"

"Yeah." My eyes scanned my surroundings. No matter what I was doing or where I was at, I always wanted to make certain that I was on my toes.

The remainder of the ride was small talk. When we made it back to the dealership, she decided that she wanted the truck, so I took her into my office and started the paperwork.

"Congratulations, Mrs. Wellington, you got yourself a brand-new G Wagon."

"It's Ms.," she corrected me.

"I'm sorry, Ms. Wellington." Her lips quirked and she extended me her hand. It was soft as cotton as I took it and shook it.

"It was a pleasure doing business with you."

Grabbing one of my cards off my desk, I handed it to her and said, "Give me a call if you need anything else."

"I just might take you up on that offer," she said, easing the card from my clutches. I stood there, observing her as she strutted out of my office.

"Mr. Blanco?" Maya poked her head into my office. "Your grandmother is on line one."

Nodding, I sat back down at my desk and picked up my phone. "Hey, Ma. You good?"

CHAPTER EIGHT
COCO
THE FOLLOWING DAY

I gazed at the empty seat across from me at the dinner table. Honey had been gone and settled into her new home. I missed her like crazy around here. Everyone else went on about their lives as if everything was normal, meanwhile, I was going insane with the distance between my twin and me. Sure enough, I was able to go visit her whenever I wanted to, but it wasn't the same as running into her room whenever I needed her. Adjusting to her being gone was hard.

"Coco?" Ma called my name, snapping me from my thoughts.

"Huh?" I focused on her as she sat toward the head of the dinner table next to Daddy.

"You haven't touched your food since you sat down. Are you okay?"

"Are y'all really going to sit here and act as if everything is alright when Honey's over there being treated like only God knows how?"

"Honey is fine. If there was something wrong, she would

have called. Eat your food," Daddy spoke up, and I rolled my eyes.

"You call her being fine being forced to marry some stranger 'cause of him!" I pointed in Dash's direction, and he stopped mid-mouth with his spoon. His eyes shifted from me to Daddy.

"Dash knows he messed up. He tried to right his wrongs. There's nothing that we can do about it now, Coco."

Boom!

I slammed my hand down on the table and my bowl and utensils clattered. "That's a lie and you know it! You're the fucking governor! There's something you can do!"

"Coco, watch your mouth," Ma said as Daddy glared at me.

"It's not as easy as you think it is. Those people are dangerous. If there was something I could do, I would have done it by now. Do you really think that I want her in their hands?"

Tears blinded my eyes. My vibrating phone grabbed my attention. Looking down on the table, I saw it was a text message from Marcia.

Sup chick? I was trying to see if you wanted to go to this party with me. I tried asking Honey but haven't heard anything back from her and I really don't want to go by myself.

My eyes darted over to my family who were eating as if nothing had just transpired. Going back to my phone, I replied, *Yeah. Be ready in an hour.*

I lifted from the table and all eyes fell on me. "Where are you going?" Ma questioned me.

"I've seem to have lost my appetite," I told her and marched away from the table.

Dialing Honey's number, I placed the phone to my ear to make sure she was okay. If she wasn't responding to Marcia, I could only think the worst.

"Hey," she dryly answered.

"You good? Marcia told me that she tried calling you but you didn't answer."

Sighing, she replied, "I'm fine. I just didn't feel like explaining anything to her."

"So you haven't told her about you getting married?"

"I haven't told anyone, Co."

"I still can't believe this," I said as I entered my bedroom. "I know there's something that Daddy can do, he just don't want to do it."

"He told me the only way out this contract is if something happens to Law."

Peeking out my bedroom, I eased the door closed and whispered, "Please tell me you're not thinking about doing something to him."

"I don't know."

"Are you trying to go to jail?"

"No, but I don't know if I'll survive over here."

"Is he doing anything to you?"

"No. I don't even see him like that. I spend all my time alone when I'm here."

"That's awful."

"Tell me about it, but I don't think I'd want it any other way. He's a monster, Co."

"I really hate this for you."

"How about we talk about something else. What are you doing?"

"I'm actually about to find something to put on so I can go out with Marcia. It was better than sitting here in the house with their fake asses."

"Go and have fun. Text me and let me know when you made it back home so I'll know that you're safe."

"Okay."

Disconnecting the call, I placed my phone on the charger

and went into my walk-in closet to find something to toss on. I found this cute ass brown, hooded tube dress and went with that. Tossing my dress on the bed, I grabbed some panties and bra then went into the bathroom to take a shower. The dress I settled on wasn't anything that I'd normally wear, especially since there was a plunging neckline. It was a dress that Honey bought one time and didn't like the way it fit her so she gave it to me. I'd never worn it before and just tossed it into the back of the closet.

After taking a shower, I got dressed and braided my hair in a French braid. It was cute as fuck with my outfit. Grabbing my phone off the charger, I saw it was nearing eight. I needed to get out of there so that I could go pick Marcia up. Marcia had her own car, but whenever we went out, she liked to ride with us so she didn't have to worry about getting home safely.

"Gladys!" I called for one of the maids on my floor and she appeared in the doorway. "Can you let them know that I need a driver?"

"Yes, ma'am."

Trotting over to my dresser, I grabbed my miniature Steve Madden purse and exited the room. By the time I made it downstairs and out the door, there was a truck sitting there waiting for me. The driver got out and opened the back door for me. "Where to?" he asked as I slipped into the seat.

"I need to pick up Marcia, then we'll let you know exactly where we're going." She didn't tell me where the party was taking place, only asked if I wanted to go, therefore, I wasn't able to tell him where we were going. Nodding, he shut the door behind me and climbed into the driver's seat.

Marcia lived out on Woodley Road with her mama. Since she was in college, she wanted to save money for once she graduated then planned on getting her own place. As we approached her house, I shot her a text to let her know we were pulling up. We weren't even in the driveway a hot second before she exited the house with a frown.

Reaching over, I opened the door for her and asked, "What's wrong?"

"Ma on her good bullshit tonight. That woman has been drinking ever since eight this morning. All she wanna do is bitch about every lil thing. I swear I can't wait to get out of here," she said and slammed the door behind her.

"I talked to Honey," I blurted in hopes it would cheer her up.

"Wait? Don't y'all stay in the same house? Why are you talking like you haven't seen her or something?"

After we got kidnapped in front of her, we didn't really go into detail about exactly what happened that day. I only told her that we were fine and it had something to do with Dash and that it was nothing that she had to worry about, and she finally left it alone. Nine times out of ten, she was about to get angry once I told her that Honey was getting married and no longer lived with us.

"That's kinda not true anymore."

Marcia's head snapped in my direction. "What the hell are you talking about?"

"Honey's getting married." I ripped the band-aid off and felt slightly better now that I was no longer holding on to that secret.

"What!" Saliva sprayed from Marcia's mouth. "Hold up. Hold up. How the hell is she getting married? She wasn't even dating anyone."

"You're right about that, but thanks to our daddy and Dash, she's marrying someone she doesn't even know."

"Like one of those arranged marriage movies?"

"Definitely, but it's much worse than that. They aren't good people."

"Who is it?"

"Law Blanco."

"Law!" Marcia pressed the back of her hand against her forehead and fake fainted. "That man fine as fuck. Shit, if she don't wanna marry him, I damn sure will. And he's fucking paid. Y'all crazy. I'd quit school if I bagged a nigga like that."

"That's beside the point, Marcia. She doesn't want to do it and I don't think it's right they are forcing her to."

"Where to?" the driver finally asked after sitting there listening to us gossip.

"Oh, sorry. Halcyon Apartments," Marcia answered and turned her attention back to me. "When's the wedding?"

Shrugging, I replied, "I don't know. Sometime in the spring. They haven't really officially set a date for it yet."

"Y'all know I have to be in it. Maybe I can find my future husband at this wedding."

"You seem to be the only person excited about it," I said, mumbling, folding my arms over my chest and slumping back against the seat.

"C'mon, Coco. Honey's living a real-life movie right now. She might even end up falling for him. Who knows, that man just might be her soulmate. Y'all shouldn't try to be so against it. Just wait it out and see how everything unfolds," she said and pulled out her phone. The light from the screen illuminated her face as she scrolled. "I'm kinda salty that y'all took this long to let me know what was going on though. Thought we were better than that."

"We are. I thought Honey had told you 'til tonight."

"Uh huh," she replied, not even looking up from her phone.

The remainder of the ride to Halcyon was silent. When the driver pulled into the complex, Marcia told him where to go. He parked the truck and got out to open the door for us. The music could be heard coming from the building before we fully reached it. There was no doubt in my mind the police wasn't gon' shut it down soon.

Marcia grabbed me by the hand and led me upstairs to an apartment. She turned the knob, and the door was unlocked. Shit was unsafe if you asked me. We entered the party and I fanned the thick smoke cloud in front of my face and coughed. There were so many people standing around the living room that I was surprised they even fit in there.

"Who's party is this?" I asked Marcia as I shut the door behind me. That should have been one of the first questions I asked her before we even got here.

"Stevie from school."

"How come you didn't tell me that before we got here?" Had she, I probably wouldn't have agreed to even come. Stevie was rude and mean. I avoided him at all costs.

"It'll be fine." Marcia gripped me by the hand and led me toward the kitchen. There was no way she was gon' be here long without getting something to drink.

When we stepped into the kitchen, I saw the counter was filled with nothing but bottles and plastic cups. A few people hung around in there socializing. Marcia grabbed the Patrón bottle and poured herself a shot. My eyes roamed the kitchen as she fixed herself a mixed drink. The guy standing in the corner eyes landed on me, and he leaned over whispering something into the guy's ear next to him. I hugged myself, feeling as if I was standing there naked as the day I was born.

"Let's go," Marcia said, placing her cup to her lips. I followed her out the kitchen and we bumped right into Stevie.

He gazed at me with this smug expression. Stevie was tall as fuck, looking as if he should have been on the basketball team or something. His hair was in a curly taper. Stroking his goatee, he licked his lips and said, "I see you made it and you brought one of those fine ass friends of yours."

"Back the hell up, Stevie. We're only here to party. Nobody wants your ass," Marcia told him and shoved him out of our path.

We made it back to the living room where everyone else was. Marcia found us a place to sit in the corner of the room in between some awkward looking chick, who was dressed in all black as if she was gothic, and this guy.

Most of the party, I remained glued to the couch. Marcia was having the time of her life and that's all that really mattered. Getting up from the couch, I grabbed her by the forearm and told her, "I'll be right back. I'm going to the bathroom."

"Let me come with you."

"No, it's fine. I'll be right back. If I'm gone too long, come looking for me."

Marcia nodded and I treaded away in search of the bathroom. When I found it, I saw there were three other people standing in line to use it. I made my way behind them and bounced on my tippytoes. *Lord, please don't let me use the bathroom on myself and embarrass myself in this party.*

The door opened and the next person went inside. It took about ten minutes for me to make it into the bathroom. Shutting the door behind me, I locked it and hurriedly squatted over the toilet. I sighed, as my pee seeped into the toilet. Once I was done, I wiped, flushed, washed my hands and proceeded to exit the bathroom. Soon as I opened the door, Stevie was standing there with a smirk on his face.

"Can you please move?"

"Why you be acting like you're better than everyone else?"

"I don't know what you're talking about." I went to shove him, but he caught me by the wrists and pushed me back into the bathroom. "Can you get the fuck out of my way?" He shut the door behind him. My palms began to clam, and my heart palpitated. "Stevie, I'm not playing with you. Let me out of this bathroom. Marcia is gon' come looking for me soon."

"I be seeing you and your sister 'round campus. You're real pretty, but I'm sure you hear that all the time." I pressed my back firmly against the wall behind me in between the toilet and the tub. "Word on the streets is that y'all a couple virgins."

Hugging myself, I replied, "Why does that even matter to you?"

The tip of his index finger stroked my cheek, and I cringed. "You're pure. Innocent, and I wanna take that innocence."

"Okay, get out my way." I shoved him and he pushed me back against the wall. My breathing labored. "This isn't funny, Stevie. Let me out of here."

"Honey!" Marcia called from outside the door then there was a knock. My eyes shot to it. His musty hand covered my mouth before I was able to respond.

"She not in here," he shouted back. I mumbled underneath his grip as if she was gon' be able to hear me over the loud music. His face neared mine and nose nestled my cheek. I kneed him in the dick. He doubled over and groaned. I moved around him for the door, but he caught me by the hood of my dress and slung me back.

Wham!

My cheek stung from the back hand slap. One swift move, he yanked the front of my dress and ripped it further. "Help!" I screamed in hopes someone would hear me, knowing damn well no one was about to come in here and save me. Everyone out there was wasted and was too busy focusing on passing out.

"Shut the fuck up," he said and pushed me back into the wall with his hand covering my mouth. His free hand slithered up my thigh and my heart dropped to the depths of my stomach. This wasn't the way I wanted to lose my virginity. I wanted to marry the man of my dreams and have him take it 'cause we were in love with each other. It's silly to some, but that's my fantasy.

Boom!

The door flew in off the hinges behind us and I saw *him* standing there. His eyes were low and dark. His jaws clenched together. Chest heaving. Marcia poked her head around him and said, "I thought you said she wasn't in here, fucking liar! Get off her!" and rushed into the bathroom. Stevie jumped back but before he was able to dart out of there, he grabbed him by the collar of his shirt and tossed him out of the bathroom like a rag doll. Marcia shielded me with her body so no one was able to see my naked breasts.

"Not only do you owe me fucking money, but you like to touch shit that don't belong to you," he said over him as he whipped his gun from his waistline and bashed Stevie across the face with it. I winced because that had to hurt.

"Streets, please!" Stevie begged before he was struck again. I find it funny how he was pleading not to get his ass kicked but wouldn't hear mine when I was asking him to leave me alone. Stevie always gave off this weird vibe, which was probably why I didn't want to fuck with him in the first place. The nigga was a rapist, and I could only imagine what would have happened had Streets not come in there and saved me.

"Where the fuck is my money?" Streets asked him as he lifted his hand back, getting ready to strike him again.

"I—I need more time."

Streets chuckled and stroked his neatly trimmed goatee. "You need more time?..." His eyes roamed around the crowd that formed to watch what was going on. None of them had common sense because why hadn't they ran out of there, especially after seeing him wave around a gun? "...You're throwing a fucking party. Looks like you got money to burn to me. You can either give me my shit now or you can have a couple more days, but you gon' be left with lead in yo' ass."

"Okay! Okay!"

Streets straightened his posture and jerked Stevie up from the floor by the collar of his shirt. He staggered toward the bedrooms. Streets unbuttoned his black shirt and handed it to Marcia before treading down the hallway behind him. Marcia turned and handed me the shirt. I slipped it on and buttoned it up then exited the bathroom behind her. My head snapped in Streets' direction as he stepped into a bedroom and shut the door behind him. Everyone else in the party went back to their business as if nothing happened. Marcia gripped me by the hand and led me toward the door.

"I'm so sorry that happened to you," she said as we took the stairs down to the truck that was still parked, waiting for us. All I could think about was what Streets was up there doing. I didn't even get the chance to thank him for saving me. The driver got out the truck and opened the door for us.

"It's fine. I'm just glad he showed up when he did." We climbed into the truck and I caught a whiff of Streets' cologne. I couldn't quite figure out what the brand was, but I'd smelled it before, and it smelled amazing. The entire way back to Marcia's house, I kept stealing whiffs of Streets. I was going to have to figure out how to reach him so I could properly thank him for saving me.

CHAPTER NINE
STREETS
A COUPLE DAYS LATER

I sat there on the edge of my bed, gazing out in space in my bedroom. My alarm had gone off twenty minutes ago to wake me, but I was already woke. Thoughts of the other night kept haunting me. Stevie was slimy and was never gon' be able to get a loan from our family again. That nigga was really 'bout to rape Coco. She was gorgeous as fuck, but that didn't give him the right to place his hands where they didn't belong.

That night when I came in the apartment in search of Stevie, I was shocked to see him in there throwing a fucking party when he owed us money. The nigga had been dodging phone calls and since he couldn't be polite enough to pick up the phone, I had to come pay him a visit. Had he kept his fucking hands to himself, he wouldn't have been left there with two broken wrists.

Getting up from the bed, I sauntered into the bathroom to handle my hygiene. It was another early day at Blanco's Loans. I had to go through paperwork and see exactly who owed us money so I could collect. Blanco's Loans was a normal loan company where you can take out a payday or personal loan. Only people that were bold came to the back room to discuss something much larger than they could receive out front.

People who normally got the much larger loans were sometimes desperate as fuck. They were willing to agree to any terms as long as they were able to get their hands on the funds. Not everyone that walked through that door with the urgency for cash was approved. We tended to turn away several people a week. People like Stevie who kept coming back 'til I finally gave in and gave him the money. I bet when he made that visit to the emergency room that night, he wished he'd never stepped foot in our establishment.

After I was done in the bathroom, I went into the walk-in closet to find me something to put on for the day. Settling on my Brooks Brothers black slacks and gold Versace button up, I got dressed and sprayed myself with my favorite Tom Ford cologne. Swiping my phone from my nightstand, I shot John a text to let him know that I was coming down in a bit to leave.

Normally, I'd stop in the kitchen and grab a bite to eat, but I was just gon' have him stop at Chick-fil-A on the way to the store. That was one of my favorite places to grab breakfast other than Mama Ada's house. If I called her right now and told her that I was hungry, she was without a doubt gon' go in that kitchen and whip something up to eat. Despite Pops hiring her a chef and maid, she still wanted to cook her food herself. Mama Ada was old fashioned. She didn't want anyone in her kitchen but her.

When I made it out the door, John was standing there waiting for me. "Good morning, sir," left his lips as he opened the door for me.

"Good morning. I want to stop by Chick-fil-A on my way to the store," I told him and slipped into the back seat. Nodding, he shut the door and rounded the truck to his side.

The ride to Chick-fil-A was a silent one. When we arrived, I sat back while John placed my order. He knew exactly what I ate from anywhere I grabbed food from. John had been driving for me ever since I turned fourteen. He took me wherever I needed to go, whenever I needed to go somewhere. I spent more time with him than I did Pops. Shit was crazy.

Growing up, I used to want Pops to spend more time with me. If he wasn't handling business, then he was spending time with Law, grooming him to take his place. I didn't mind it, 'cause I never wanted to be head of the mafia in the first place, but he still could have divided his time between both his kids. While Law was out with Pops, I spent most of my time with Ma crunching numbers. She was the brains behind the loan company. When she passed, I begged Pops to let me take over. He wanted to have Law run everything and that shit wasn't fair. The loan company was mine. I knew everything like the back of my hand. Ma made damn sure of it.

John passed me my food, bringing me from my thoughts. He pulled out of the parking lot and headed toward the main branch of the loan company downtown. It was where I conducted most of my business. When we arrived, I saw Trina's car parked out front. *At least she had some sense.*

Getting out the truck, I entered the building and Trina shot to her feet. "I've been waiting for you to get here," she said, brushing out the wrinkles in her sweater dress.

"You do know that you could have just handed Charlene the money, right? You didn't have to speak to me directly."

"Oh, but I wanted to. I want you to know that I repaid my debt so that I don't have to worry about your friends coming back in and tearing up the place. You cost me money." Folding her arms over her chest, she pouted.

"That's what happens when you owe people. From now on, pay ya fucking debt or don't take money from people at all," I said and marched down the hallway toward my office with her directly on my heels.

"Oh, trust me, after all that shit, I don't plan on ever taking out another loan from y'all. I'll starve to death before I do that."

Chuckling, I rounded my mahogany desk and took a seat in my black throne chair. "Just give me what you owe and get the fuck out of here."

"You don't want me to wait while you count it?" Her brow arched to her hairline.

"I'on think you that stupid to short me."

"Hhhmp." Trina reached into her purse and pulled out a white envelope and slammed it down on my desk.

When I looked up from the envelope, I saw Coco standing in the doorway. "I'm sorry. I'll just come back," she said and rushed off.

Getting up from my desk, I pushed Trina out the way and went behind her. By the time I reached Coco, she had made it to her truck. The driver opened the back door for her, and I gripped her by the forearm, stopping her. "I was handling business," I felt the need to tell her. For whatever reason, I didn't want her thinking I was connected to Trina. She wasn't an ugly chick by far, but I wasn't dealing with anyone at the moment, not even her. "What are you doing here?"

"I've been looking for you so that I can thank you for the other night. I left before I was able to."

"That's no problem. He owed me money anyway." I didn't tell her that I broke the nigga's wrists before I left though. That part was done for her.

"Still, I wanted to thank you." Reaching into her yellow Birkin, she pulled out a plastic container.

"What's this?" I asked when she shoved it in my direction.

"Freshly baked chocolate chip cookies."

A smile tugged at the corner of my lips. "Freshly baked, huh? Who made 'em?"

"I did."

"You bake?"

"Among other things."

"Thanks. You really didn't have to."

"Maybe to you, I didn't, but I couldn't move on with myself without letting you know that I was thankful."

I wasn't certain if it was the sun that caused her tawny face to glow or what, but Coco beamed like a goddess standing before me. Her eyes drew me into a trance. Her glossy round lips parted and she said, "Thanks again." Closing the gap between us, she pressed her lips firmly against my cheek, causing a warm sensation down to my feet. I stood there, trapped in place as she climbed back into her truck. The driver shut the door behind her and rounded to the driver's side. They backed out their parking space and pulled off. Popping the lid on the container, my eyes focused on the perfectly shaped cookies. *How the hell did she know that chocolate chip was my favorite?* By the time I lifted my eyes, they were no longer in sight.

CHAPTER TEN
HONEY

I hugged myself right after the covers were snatched from my frame. "It's time to get up," Ma said as she yanked the curtains open and blinded the fuck out of me. Grabbing my pillow, I attempted to smother myself to hide from the sun. "You've been putting this off for far too long, Honey. We really need to get a jump on this if we're going to meet this deadline."

"Go away," I said, muffled by the pillow.

"Honey, I know you may not want to do this, but you're the one who agreed to it." Sighing, I eased the pillow from my head and sat up in bed. Ma stood at the side of the bed. "Can you get cleaned up and meet us downstairs?"

"Us?"

"Yes. Ada and the wedding planner they hired is waiting downstairs."

"Are you serious?"

"It was either that or plan all of this on your own."

"Fine."

Ma bounced out the room and I pressed the pillow against my face and screamed, "Ahhhhhh!" Taking a couple deep breaths, I pulled myself from bed and went into the bathroom to shower and brush my teeth.

By the time I made it downstairs, I found everyone sitting at the dining room table with books spread out everywhere. Ada sat at the head of the table with Ma next to her, and some middle-aged woman sat across from her.

"There's that ray of sunshine," Ada said with a huge grin. This was my second time encountering her since I'd been here. "Do you need anything before we get started?"

Shaking my head, I took the seat next to Ma. "Ada was just telling me about this talented guy from Montgomery who can make a dress for you. She showed me some of his work on his social media and he does some gorgeous work. I really think that you'll love him. Asha here agreed when she saw them."

"I'll be fine with just a white dress from Walmart."

"You'll wear no such thing. The budget for this wedding is two million dollars. You—" I choked when I heard Ada say that. Had they lost their fucking mind? Two million was a bit much for a wedding for two people who didn't even want to marry each other in the first place.

"Are you okay?" Ma turned to me and asked.

Clearing my throat, I replied, "Yes."

"As I was saying, you have a huge budget. You can spend it on your dream dress or whatever your heart desires."

"But I don't have a dream dress."

"That's fine. A lot of women don't. You can try to Google some dresses and see what style you like best and we can go from there," Asha, the wedding planner, spoke up.

"Okay, I guess."

"Ada also told me that all the family weddings happen at their estate, so we don't have to focus on a venue, but we do need to come up with a theme for your wedding."

"I need a theme? Why can't I just pick some colors and go with that?"

"These days, weddings have themes. We can search up some and see if you like any of them."

"This seems like a lot of work."

"Weddings normally are, but it's my job to make it easier. I promise it'll be smooth sailing as long as you communicate with me."

For the next couple of hours, we sat there having wedding talk. It was overwhelming and I couldn't wait to get the hell out of there. Asha had scheduled an engagement photoshoot which I thought was silly as hell, but she kept saying it was one of the most important things of the engagement. I finally agreed to it just so she could get the hell out of my face.

Once they were done, Ma ended up leaving and heading back home. Since I didn't have anything else to do for the day, I decided to call up Coco and Marcia so that we can go shopping and have lunch to catch up on everything that I'd missed the last couple days. Coco answered the FaceTime first then Marcia.

"What are y'all doing?" I asked them as I searched through the closet for something to put on. I'd been walking around the house in lounge clothes since I wasn't doing anything but meeting Ma nem downstairs.

"Nothing. I was just reading a book," Coco answered. That was one of her favorite pastimes. If one ever wanted to get her a gift, they couldn't go wrong with buying her a good book.

"I was just looking for something to eat. There's always nothing to fucking eat here," Marcia said and shut the refrigerator.

"Perfect. I was trying to see if y'all wanted to go to the mall and grab lunch. Everything's on me."

"How?" Marcia quickly answered.

"Baby, I got a black card now," I answered with a smile. If I was forced to be here, I was gon' hit their asses where it hurts.

"No fucking way." Marcia's eyes widened like saucers. "See, I told you, Coco. She's gon' be just fine."

"What's that supposed to mean?" I asked her with a frown.

"Girl, you're fucking paid now. You don't have nothing to worry about ever again in life. You're set. Coco was worried about you marrying into that family, but girl that's probably a fucking blessing. You never know what'll happen."

My mind drifted back to the first real conversation that I had with Law. I'd rather have love than money and I was being forced to spend the rest of my life without it. What kind of life is that to live?

"I don't want to talk about that anymore. Are y'all coming or what?"

"Yeah, I can come," Coco said, shutting her book and getting up from the bed. "I'll be ready in a few." Her FaceTime ended and I focused my attention on Marcia.

"Girl, you had me when you said it was on you and lunch. See you in a few," she replied and ended the video.

Finally finding what I wanted to wear, I got dressed and exited the bedroom. Law had designated a driver to me. I didn't really care because I was already used to it from Daddy. He was sitting outside in the truck when I walked out the door. Nigga must have been dozing off or something because he hadn't even noticed me walk up. He jumped when he heard the back door open and turned in my direction.

"I'm sorry," he started.

"It's fine. Can you take me to pick up my sister and best friend? We're going to Eastchase," I told him and shut the door behind me.

"Okay." He started the truck and put it in drive.

We walked around Eastchase with our shopping bags. We had been inside several stores. I couldn't even say how much money we'd spent because I wasn't checking the tags, just swiping the card.

We took the bags back to the truck and got inside. "Where y'all want to get lunch from?" I asked them, because I didn't really have a taste for anything and didn't care where we went.

"Bonefish Grill," Marcia answered with the quickness.

"Bonefish it is," I replied and settled back against the seat.

We made it to the restaurant and went inside. The hostess stopped us at the door. "How many?"

"Three," I answered her. She grabbed the menus and took us to our booth. We settled in and she took our drink orders.

As we looked over the menu, Marcia asked, "Did y'all ever figure out what y'all were doing for your birthday?"

"With the wedding planning and all, I hadn't really thought much about it. I think we should just take a vacation and call it a day."

"That sounds like a plan," Coco blurted. She didn't really want to have a party in the first place.

"I'll look at some places and shoot you some ideas and we can go from there. It'll just be a girls' trip." It'd be nice to get away from all this chaos for a while.

As we sat there and looked at the menu, my phone chimed. Picking it up, I saw it was a text message from Asha. *The photoshoot is scheduled for tomorrow afternoon.*

CHAPTER ELEVEN
LAW
THE FOLLOWING DAY

I had been trying my best to avoid all this shit. That's the exact reason why I allowed Mama Ada to help plan the wedding, so I didn't have any parts in it, but somehow, I got roped into taking fucking pictures. The day before, I received a text letting me know what time and where I needed to be to take said pictures. I tried talking to Mama Ada to get out of taking the pictures, but she claimed it was important and I needed to be there. Taking those photos meant I was gon' have to be close proximity with Honey, and I wasn't certain how to feel about that.

My driver pulled up to Shakespeare Park and opened the back door for me. When I arrived, I saw Honey's truck already there, but she wasn't inside. I followed the directions of where they wanted me to go. The first pictures were to be taken under the gazebo. As I approached, I saw Honey standing there talking to some guy with a camera. Her back was facing me. From what I could see, she wore this black, lace, mermaid gown. When she turned around, I noticed the provocative split up to her right thigh. Her hair flowed in huge curls with a part down the middle. Her makeup was light and flawless. Any man would have been lucky to be marrying Honey Hurts, but I wasn't that man.

She folded her arms over her chest and her eyes turned to slits as she glowered at me. "I take it that you're the husband. Welcome, Mr. Blanco," the photographer said and trudged in my direction with his hand extended.

"Can we just get this over with? I have somewhere to be," I said, ignoring his gesture, and stepped underneath the gazebo with Honey.

"You two look so beautiful together," Mama Ada said, grasping my attention. She didn't tell me that she was gon' be here.

"What are you doing here?" I quickly questioned her.

"I knew that you two were supposed to take pictures today. I thought that you would need this," she said, stepping to us with a tiny box in her hand. "It was your mother's." My heart stopped in my chest.

"No. I was gon' buy one."

"She would have wanted you to have it. Take it."

I bared my teeth. If I was gon' give my mama's ring to someone, it would have been someone I was in love with, not some woman I was being forced to marry for everyone else's sake.

"Please, Lawrence. It's only right. This ring has been passed down for generations. It's now your turn."

"It's really fine," Honey said, probably sensing my hesitation.

Retrieving the box, I popped it open and slipped the oval-shaped, rose-gold, diamond ring onto Honey's finger. Ironically, it fit her perfectly. "Can we just get this over with?" I asked, and Mama Ada nodded.

Taking a few steps back from the gazebo, she clasped her

hands together and pressed 'em to her lips as she watched us get in position to take pictures.

"I want to get a close up on that gorgeous ring if you two don't mind," the photographer said, stepping to us. "I have a position in mind. How about you kneel on one knee in front of Honey?" I did as I was told, getting a whiff of her perfume. This was the closest I'd ever been to her. The wind lightly blew, and tiny goosebumps coursed her arms. My eyes trailed up her arms to her slender face. "Okay, Honey. I want you to cradle Law's face."

"What?" My head snapped in his direction.

He chuckled and grabbed her by the wrists, positioning her hands over each of my ears. "There," he said, taking a step back. Her eyes bored into mine for the first time and my heart palpitated. "That's perfect." The light from the camera flashed twice. "Now let's try another position." Honey's hands swiftly dropped from my face, and I straightened my posture.

Honey stepped in front of me with her back pressed against my frame. My body tensed because I wasn't expecting her to be this close to me. My hands synced with her hips, and I noted the goosebumps trickling down on her shoulder.

"I really love you two together. You have so much chemistry," the photographer said as he snapped photos. Honey effortlessly switched positions and I fell in line with whichever one she chose. She was photogenic as hell. I could tell from her social media.

"Okay, now I just need one more. The kiss." Honey's body went rigid in my arms.

"I think that's enough," Honey quickly spoke and went to walk off, but I caught her by the wrist and pulled her into my frame. Her lips collided with mine, and I could have sworn I felt a prick in mine. Had we not taken that picture, Mama Ada was just gon' kept insisting that we did. I'd rather get the shit over now and gone 'bout my business.

"And that's a wrap," the photographer said. I released Honey and she stumbled away from me.

"You two look so beautiful together," Mama Ada said as she approached us. "I can't wait 'til the world sees these pictures."

"I still think it's pointless," I blurted, and Honey rolled her eyes. The wind blew her hair and she hugged herself.

"Lawrence, how about you give your fiancée your jacket. Can't you see that she's cold?"

"So you rather I be cold instead?"

Mama Ada shot me an evil glare. Sighing, I peeled out my jacket and handed it to Honey. She slipped it on and proceeded across the parking lot toward the trucks.

"Will it kill you to be nice to her? Honey's a sweet girl. She's beautiful and smart too. You're lucky to have ended up with someone like her."

"I keep telling y'all that I don't want anyone at all. Look where that got Pops."

"His fate doesn't have to be yours. The sooner you realize that, the better it'll be for everybody. It's cold out here. I'm going to head home." I pecked Mama Ada on the cheek and walked her back to her truck. Honey was long gone before I made it to the parking lot. I'd just have to get my coat from her later.

I helped Mama Ada into the truck and stood there 'til they were no longer in sight. Climbing into my truck, I told Fredrick, "Take me to the dealership. There's a few loose ends I need to tie up," and he shut the door.

I stood there in the parking lot, watching as the driver of the trailer pulled all of our vehicles off. "All of 'em are accounted for," TP said, and I nodded. Ever since Wick and Dash stole one of the cars, we had the drivers switch up their routes. That's something we should have been doing in the first place. We got comfortable thinking that no one was stupid enough to fuck with us. Wick's ass has been in hiding ever since the incident. Though Pops squared everything away with the Hurts, I was gon' break Wick's fucking neck whenever I caught his bitch ass. That nigga was so fucking salty that I wouldn't let him join the mafia. We had no use for his ass. He was dead weight.

"Great. Unload the cars," I instructed him.

My phone began to ring and I pulled it from my pocket. It was an unknown number. Seeing how a lot of people got a hold to my number, there was no telling who was calling me.

"Yeah?" I answered.

"Is this Lawrence Blanco?" the woman asked.

"Yes. May I ask who I'm speaking with?"

"Hey, this is Lala. You sold me that G Wagon a few days ago. It's something wrong with it. Can you come by and check it out for me?"

"I can send a wrecker and bring it in if you want me to."

"I think I'd prefer if you came by and looked at it yourself. Can you?"

My eyes darted to the trailer. They were almost done unloading the truck. TP was here and could manage for a few hours without me, so I replied, "Sure. Shoot me your address and I'm on my way," then disconnected the call.

Stepping to TP who was climbing into one of the Maseratis, I told him, "I have to run somewhere right quick, but I'll be back in a couple hours. Call if you need me."

Nodding, he shut the door and pulled toward the warehouse. I trotted to the front of the parking lot where Fredrick was parked. Soon as I made it to the truck, Lala's text came through with her address. I told Fredrick her address and got into the truck.

When we arrived at Lala's house, her truck was backed up to the garage door next to a white BMW 750. He parked on the side of the street and opened the back door for me. I climbed out and went up to her front door then rang the doorbell. Lala wasted no time opening the door as if she was standing there waiting for me. A huge smile adorned her face. She stood there in these purple yoga pants and a matching sports bra. Lala's body was insane. I had to train my eyes to hers to keep 'em from wandering.

"Let me grab my keys," she said and turned, bouncing her ass hard as fuck with every step she took. Without a doubt, she was baiting the shit out of me, and I wasn't certain how much longer it was gon' be before I caved. I hadn't had any pussy since Honey arrived at my house. I had no plans of fucking her ass either.

Lala came back to the door and I followed her over to the truck. She opened the driver's door and slipped into the seat. I stood there as she placed the key in the ignition and tried to start it, but nothing happened.

"Hhmm, that's strange," I said, stroking my chin, trying to think of what reason why her truck wouldn't start.

"It just started doing that this morning. It was working fine yesterday when I went to Walmart and bought a few car accessories."

"Let me give it a try. I'm no mechanic but I know a lil some," I told her, and she stepped out the truck. I took her place and went to turn the key over when I noticed this diamond ring around the ignition. "This your problem right here. Don't you know that these things are no good? They stop your car from cranking," I told her and pulled it off.

Soon as I took that piece off and turned the key, the truck started.

"Wow. I really didn't know that. I saw it and thought it was so cute." Her face turned beet red. "That's crazy. If they're such an issue, why make 'em?"

"I don't know."

"Thanks for taking time out of your busy schedule to come by here and see what I wanted. You want something to drink or something to eat as a thank you?"

"No. I'm good," I told her and turned her truck off then handed her the keys.

"You sure? I made some lasagna. It's more than enough to share with you. As a matter of fact, I'm not taking no for an answer." Gripping me by the hand, she led me to the front door. "You're out there working hard, you should put something on your stomach." I entered her house behind her and she didn't stop walking 'til we made it to the kitchen. "Have a seat." She gestured toward the kitchen table. It was glass with four black tufted chairs sitting at it.

I took a seat in one of the chairs and observed her as she fixed a plate, warmed it and brought it over to me. "I'll fix you some lemonade," she said and went over to the cabinet to grab a glass. I watched her ass lift as she reached up and grabbed one of the cups. My dick bricked and I pushed it down. If I didn't get my ass out of here and soon, I was gon' have her ass bent the fuck over this got damn table.

"I'd love to stay and eat this delicious looking food, but I really should get back," I said and rose to my feet.

Lala darted in my direction and pinned me against the table. Her breasts stroked my lower chest as she eyed me. "Why are you trying to leave so soon? What's wrong? Did I do or say something wrong?" She was fiending for this dick. Anyone with two eyes could see that shit. If I didn't know any better, I'd think that whole bullshit 'bout her truck not starting was staged.

"No. I don't think you know exactly what you're getting yourself into here."

"Why you say that?"

"We both know that you didn't just call me here 'bout no truck."

Her fingertips grazed my arm and she responded, "Then why else did I call you here?"

Wrapping my hand firmly around her neck, I backed her against the nearest wall. Her heart beat so rapidly against her chest that I could feel it throbbing. "You want this dick so bad, suck it." Still gripping her neck, I eased her down to her knees. Lala lustfully gazed up at me as she undid my belt and whipped my dick out. Wrapping her hand 'round my dick, she twirled the tip of her tongue 'round the head before coughing up a mouth filled of salvia and spit on my shit. Lala massaged her saliva into my dick as she shoved it into her mouth. Releasing her neck, I gripped a hand full of her braids and guided her up and down on my shit.

My free hand slammed against the wall above her head and mine tilted backward. Lala sucked and slurped on my shit, making humming noises. My toes curled in my shoes, feeling my nut rise.

"Fuck," I groaned.

Her mouth made a popping sound when she released my dick. Lala continued to massage it as she looked up at me and asked, "You like that?"

"Shut the fuck up and just suck the shit," I told her and shoved my dick right back into her mouth. She gagged on it, supplying more saliva. Shit was driving me insane. I loved myself some sloppy ass head. "Right there," I said, and she kept her rhythm, and I quickly released my seeds down her throat.

Releasing Lala, I shoved my dick back into my pants, and she got up off her knees. "No dick?" she asked.

"Maybe next time. I really gotta get outta here. I'll be in touch though." Without uttering another word, I exited her house.

CHAPTER TWELVE
JADEN "WICK" PETERMAN
A WEEK LATER

I brushed my hand across my hair as I paced the floor. My mind had been going a million miles a minute for the last hour.

Boom! Boom! Boom!

My frame halted, and I faced the front door. Rushing to it, I yanked it open and pulled Dash into the door.

"What took you so fucking long?" I questioned him.

"Why you so antsy? The fuck going on?"

"I asked you here 'cause I have a plan that I wanted you to hear."

"Nah." Dash's hand lifted, halting me. "I ain't trying to hear no more of yo' fucking brilliant ass ideas. The last one you came to me with, caused Honey to end up having to marry someone she don't even know. You're not screwing us over again. Whatever the fuck that plan is, you can keep that shit to yourself."

He turned and grabbed the doorknob, but I jumped in front of him. "You haven't even heard what the idea is first, and you're already against it."

"I ain't trying to hear what it is either. Move." He shoved me and I stumbled a lil bit. Dash exited my apartment, and I rushed out behind him.

"Fine, be that way! When I come up off this shit, don't come crawling to me!" I yelled behind him and slammed the door. Pulling my phone out, I called D'mon to let him know what happened. D'mon was another one of my friends that I'd known since I was in elementary school. He was more down with me than Dash, probably 'cause he related to me more. D'mon didn't have some rich daddy to fall back on. We both were getting shit out the mud. Dash was always gon' be set 'cause his family was gon' make damn sure of it.

Governor Hurts came from a long line of politicians. They basically ran the city of Montgomery with the Blanco family backing 'em. Governor Hurts had his hands in all sorts of investments and they were paying extremely well. That's one of the reasons why Dash wasn't really hurting for shit. I, on the other hand, came from nothing and didn't really have shit going for myself aside from my charming looks. College wasn't for me. I hated everything 'bout school. But fast money... that shit had my name all over it, and I was willing to do whatever it takes to ensure I got my hands on it. That included the heist I was setting up that could change my life forever.

"Yeah?" D'mon finally answered the phone. For a second, I thought the shit was gon' ring out to voicemail.

"Damn, everybody playing with my fucking time today, ain't it?"

"What are you talking 'bout?" he shot back.

"Nothing. Dash's out."

"Are you serious? Where the hell we gon' get the third manpower from?"

"Don't worry 'bout it. I think I have someone in mind."

"I damn sure hope it's someone you trust. We don't have

time for someone walking 'round here running their fucking mouth."

"Do I look stupid to you? Just be ready by four thirty so we can get this shit over with." Ending the call, I swiped my keys off the end table and exited the house.

FOUR THIRTY

I chewed on the inside of my jaw as we sat across the street and eyed the building. My heart skipped beats in my chest. The shit we were 'bout to pull off was gon' have to go as planned or else all of us could lose our lives.

"You good?" D'mon questioned me as he slapped a clip into his pistol. One would think that we would have brought something a tad bit more powerful than that shit. Though I'd been staking out the place for weeks, I was never able to go into the back and didn't know exactly what type of weapons they had back there, if any.

"Yeah." I wasn't 'bout to let him know that my nerves were all over the place. He'd call me a lil bitch. "Let's get this shit over with," I said and pulled my mask down over my face. After staking out the place, I realized what time the place was empty, which was near closing every day. That was the best time to go in there. We'd have less casualties and most likely be able to get in and out. At the end of the day was when they'd clean out the drawers and count the money before placing it into the safe.

We ran across the parking lot and entered the building. There was one person standing at the window waiting to be helped. Two people stood behind the glass. There was normally three, but the other went home every day 'round three thirty. Sometimes Streets would have his ass in the back office, but that was normally earlier in the day. One of the chicks behind the counter spotted me and patted the other one, gaining her attention.

Soon as I saw her reach for the panic button, I aimed my gun at the woman standing at the counter. "Press it and I'll splatter her brains all over that fucking window." Her hands swiftly went up into the air. "That's what the fuck I thought. So this is what's gon' happen. One of y'all gon' walk over and kindly open that door for me. Preferably you," I said, pointing at the one closest to the door.

"Do you know who you're robbing?" she asked me as if I gave a fuck.

"That's the reason why we're standing here. You can thank your boss later. For now, open the fucking door."

"We were told to never open that door for anyone who isn't a Blanco, and even then they should have a key."

I grabbed the woman in front of me and placed my gun against her temple. Her hands shot in the air, and she squealed. "We can do this shit the easy way or the hard way."

"Please," the woman begged, knowing her life was at stake.

"Don't you dare open that door. Who's to say that he won't kill us once he gets back here," the other woman said.

"Honestly, I don't want to kill anyone. I just want the cash and I'll be the hell out of here. I can kill her and then wait y'all asses out and kill you if you don't want to open that door. Do what's right and open it. We all want to make it out of here alive today."

"Fuck," the girl said and yanked the door open.

"Charlene!" the other one screamed her name. I released the woman and made my way behind the counter.

"Now which one of you gon' open that safe for me back there in that office?"

"We don't know the code."

"You really gon' stand there and lie to my face like that? I see y'all wanna do shit the hard way." Turning back to the glass, my eyes locked with D'mon who had his gun trained on the hostage. I nodded and he shot her in the shoulder. The two women in the room with me screamed. Facing them, I said, "The next one gon' go in her fucking face if y'all keep playing with me. One of y'all open the fucking safe."

"Okay! Okay!" the smart-mouth one said and stepped in my direction. I shoved her out the room and faced D'mon.

"Tie the other one up," I instructed and picked up the duffel off the floor. I didn't even have to walk out of here with the entire safe. All I needed was whatever filled this bag up.

We went toward a door in the back, and she punched a code in. It unlocked and she pushed the door in. It must be Streets' office. Rounding the desk to the huge steel safe, she punched in a code and the door popped open.

"Move." I shoved her to the side, not knowing what was gon' be in that safe. For all I knew, there could be weapons and she could turn around and shoot my stupid ass in the face.

I opened the door and my mouth hit the floor. The safe was stuffed with cash. One would think since they were the mafia that they'd keep most of this money elsewhere. Easy lick.

I stuffed the bag with cash 'til I couldn't get any more in there. Once I was done, I zipped the bag up and grabbed shawty by the forearm. Yanking the extension cord out the wall, I tightly wrapped it 'round her wrists and shoved her out the room. Draping the bag over my shoulder, I exited behind her and took her ass right on back to her friend.

"Did you get it?" D'mon quickly asked me.

I patted the bag and trotted toward the door. "What about her?" D'mon asked.

"Leave her. She can call for help once we gone. If I were you, I'd wait at least five minutes before you call someone," I told her and exited the door with D'mon on my trail.

CHAPTER THIRTEEN
COCO
SAME DAY

Ever since I found out that Honey was really going to go through with that wedding, I had been trying my best to figure out what exactly I can gift her. It was hard when a person had damn near everything they wanted. See, had I asked Honey, she probably would have told me something on the lines of her freedom, and that's something I couldn't provide right now. Trust me, I tried.

After much thought, I figured that I'd gift them a playlist. A sweet one that they can listen to and hopefully help with their love life. Since I didn't know anything about Law, I decided to ask Streets for help. I had gone by the loan place earlier in search of him, but he wasn't working there today. I ended up having to call Honey for a favor to find out where he was. She kept asking me all sorts of questions about why I was looking for him in the first place, so I lied. I told her about how he saved me that night and wanted to thank him. Had I told her the truth, it would have ruined everything.

My driver pulled up to a gate and rang the bell. "Who is it?" a voice came through the speaker.

Letting the window down, I scooted over and leaned my head out and replied, "It's Coco Hurts. I'm here to see Streets."

My eyes wandered the bronze gate as I waited for a response. Just as I fixed my mouth to tell the driver to leave, the gate buzzed. He drove through and I peeped the house that I was at the day all of us were taken hostage. How could I forget this place? It was beautiful as hell on the outside, but the inside gave me chills. It reeked of trauma in the halls. Honestly, I didn't understand how they were still living here.

The driver pulled down the long driveway to the door and Streets stood at the wooden double doors dressed in a tailored black suit. His silk, navy blue button up had the top buttons undone. A Blanco Cuban chain danced around his neck.

Soon as the truck came to a halt in front of the porch, he took the couple steps down and opened the door for me. "What are you doing here?" he questioned and extended his hand for me to take.

"I needed your help," I said and turned to grab the Taste food bag off the seat. "I brought lunch too."

His brow arched. "Need my help with what?"

"Well, I've been trying to figure out what to get Honey and Law for their wedding." Streets chuckled and I frowned. "What's funny?"

"We normally just hand out cash and call it a day."

"Well, I don't want to give her cash. I want to do something meaningful, and I thought it'd be nice if I were to make them a playlist, but I don't know the first thing about Law. I don't know what type of music he likes, so I need your help. Where should we set up at?" I asked him and strutted toward the front door.

I stepped inside the house and was in awe. Despite the things that took place here, their home was gorgeous as hell. Beautiful artwork lined the white walls.

"Where am I going?"

Streets took the food bag away from me and headed for the staircase. My fingertips brushed the gold railing as I followed him up to the second floor. A huge diamond and gold chandelier hung from the ceiling over the foyer. "This house is gorgeous."

"I would say thanks, but it's not mine."

"You don't live here?"

"No, but I still have a room here."

We entered a bedroom that looked as if it was fit for a king. The gigantic black tufted bed sat in the center of the room with gold and black bedding. To the right of me was a living room with a black leather sofa set and huge television on the wall. If I had to take a guess, it had to be over seventy-five inches. He led me over to the living room area and we took a seat.

"I hate to burst your bubble, but Law isn't really the music type."

"Who doesn't love music?"

"Law's ass." He chortled. "I can still help you with a playlist if you want me to."

"Okay." He sat the food down on the coffee table, and I pulled out my phone. "I've already been looking at some songs. You want to hear them?"

Streets nodded and I started the first song on the playlist: Teeks' "First Time" began to play. He removed his jacket and neatly folded it onto the back of the chair before taking a seat on the couch next to me. I observed him as he sat there with his elbows on his thighs and leaned forward. His scent trickled up my nostrils, and I shut my eyes and took a huge whiff.

Every time I encountered this man, he smelled so fucking good. It should have been a crime for him to look and smell this amazing. Whatever chick bagged him was gon' be lucky as fuck, that's if he wasn't already spoken for. We hadn't been in each other's presence long enough for me to know if he was single or not. I certainly hadn't been digging around to find out. I could have easily asked Marcia about it. She seemed to know everyone's business.

"Coco?" Streets called my name, bringing me from my dangerous thoughts. I faced him. "I was saying that I like that song. It might be good for her to walk down the aisle to or for their first dance."

"You don't think that they'll be telling a lie to everyone if they did that? Let's face it, we all know they aren't in love with each other and honestly, I don't know if they'd ever get there."

"Law isn't an easy person to try and get through to. He's never wanted to be in a committed relationship ever since our mama got killed."

My hand covered my mouth, and I gasped. "Oh my God, I'm so sorry. I didn't know that. That must be so... so... sad. I can't imagine my life without my mama."

"It has its days." He relaxed back against the couch and his eyes lowered. "She was our everything. I looked up to her. She always wanted more for us. Out of all the bullshit we dealt with, she was the calm, if that makes sense."

"I definitely get it. Y'all didn't make the best first impression."

"Sorry 'bout that. We did what we had to do. A lot of the shit that we do, I don't really agree with but it's necessary."

"Is it though?" My head cocked to the side.

"You don't understand 'cause you're not from this life."

"Maybe you're right. I still don't agree with it though. Let's get back to the music."

We searched up some more songs for the next couple of hours while we ate our food. I kept stealing glances at Streets. It was hard being in his proximity and not admiring him. Maybe had we met under different circumstances, and he had a change in lifestyle, we could have pursued something together.

"I have to get going," I said, shooting to my feet and grabbing my coat.

"Do you have everything you need?"

"I think so. Thanks for helping," I said. Streets lifted to his feet. Our faces were mere inches apart as he straightened his posture. My breath caught in my throat. "Thanks!" I said again and rushed out of there with my tail tucked.

When I made it back out to the truck, I dialed Marcia's number. She wasted no time answering the phone.

"I got a question. What do you know about Streets Blanco?"

"Ms. Coco, what are you questioning me about Streets for? Do you have a crush on him?"

"No!" I quickly lied. In the short time we spent together, I was starting to feel a tingle of some sort for him. Maybe it was because he'd saved me. I don't know. Whatever it was, I needed to shake it, but I couldn't help myself from pondering on him.

"I don't really know much about him. He's softer than Law. I can tell you that."

"What do you mean by soft?"

"Don't get me wrong, Streets is just about as deadly as his brother, but he has a softer side. He's kinda sweet. He's always been nice every time I've seen him."

"Okay, I guess that's a good thing."

"Yo' lil hot ass want Streets, don't you?"

"I don't know. I've spent a lil time with him. He don't seem like he'd go for my type."

"Are you crazy? Girl, you're fucking smart and hot. Any man would die to have someone like you."

"A virgin though, Marcia? I tell that man that I'm celibate, he's more than likely to run for the hills."

"You'll never know unless you try and find out."

"I guess you're right."

"I know I am."

"Lunch tomorrow?" I asked her as the truck pulled out the driveway.

"Sure, but I'm picking the place."

"'Kay."

CHAPTER FOURTEEN
STREETS

I stood there, watching Coco from my bedroom window as her truck pulled out the driveway. It was shocking seeing her show up here like that. My phone chimed and I slipped it from my pocket. Seeing that the store was calling, I immediately answered. "Yeah?"

"Someone just robbed us!" Charlene screamed into the phone.

"Wait, what!" I marched over and grabbed my coat and exited the bedroom.

"We called 911 'cause one of the customers got shot. They forced me to open the safe. I'm not sure exactly how much money he took. I haven't gotten the chance to count it yet."

"I ain't worried 'bout the money. Long as y'all are straight. I'm on my way there. Let me hit up Law right quick," I told her and disconnected the call.

As I exited the house, John got out and opened the back door for me. Law picked up soon as my ass touched the seat.

"Wassup?"

"Someone just robbed the main store."

"What the fuck you mean somebody just robbed it?" The tone in his voice quickly shifted.

"I haven't made it there yet, but that's what Charlene just called and told me. I'm on my way there to check on everything."

"I'll meet you there." The line went dead.

It was crazy for someone to get bold and rob us. First Wick and Dash stole one of our cars and now this shit. No one had ever had the balls to fuck with our shit and now it was as if everyone wanted to get a taste of fucking with us. We had to hurry up and nip this shit in the bud before anything else happened.

John pulled up to the building and flashing lights were everywhere. A woman was being pulled out of the building on a gurney. Tires screeched behind me and I saw it was Law. He hopped out the truck before I was even able to get out. A mug rested on his face as he made his way into the building.

"Did you see who it was?" he asked before his foot was even in the door good.

"No. They were wearing masks but it was two of them," Tiffany answered.

"Why the fuck you opened the door? You know you aren't supposed to open the fucking door." His eyes turned to slits. Charlene rubbed up and down her arm and diverted her eyes to the floor.

"He was gon' kill the customer. We had to open the door," Charlene answered for her.

Law's fist crashed into the wall alongside him. "I don't give a damn! Y'all know you ain't supposed to open that fucking door under no fucking circumstances!" he barked and marched out of there with me directly behind him.

"That was a lil harsh, don't you think?"

"In training, they were instructed not to open that fucking door."

"They did what they thought was best. Calm down."

"How much did they get away with?"

"We don't know yet."

"Tell them to get on it. I'm going to the governor's house."

"Wait, why?" I caught him by the forearm and asked.

"Dash got something to do with this shit. I know he does and he gon' fucking pay for fucking with us," he replied and yanked away from me.

"I'm coming with you. You aren't going over there by yourself." I was afraid to allow Law to do that because there was no telling what the hell he was gon' do once he got there.

Without uttering another word, he jumped into his truck and peeled out of there. I got into mine and went behind him. As John pulled off, I shot Charlene a text letting her know that once everything was situated at the store to go count and see exactly how much money was stolen.

We arrived at the governor's house and Law jumped from the truck before it came to a complete stop. He marched upstairs and the guards opened the door for him. "Dash!" he barked and took the stairs up to the second floor. "Dash!" Law began to open every single door in search of Dash's ass.

"What's going on?" Honey stepped out of one of the rooms and asked.

"Where the fuck is Dash?" Law questioned her as he opened another door and came up empty-handed.

"I don't know. You want to tell me why you're screaming his name like that? What's going on? What has he done now?"

"You really don't know where he is?" I asked her in hopes that she'd be honest with me. If Law didn't find Dash and soon, there was no telling what the fuck he was gon' do.

"I haven't seen him. I just got here not too long ago. I forgot one of my school books and came to pick it up," she responded and lifted the book in the air. "I have to study for a test. I can try calling his phone and see if he answers."

Just as she said that, Dash jogged upstairs with an apple up to his lips. Law's fist went across his face, knocking the apple to the floor before he could get a full bite.

"What the hell, man!" Dash yelled and eyed his apple on the floor.

"I'm gon' beat the yellow out yo' ass," Law warned and swung on him again.

"What the hell is going on?" Mrs. Hurts stepped out a room down the hallway and asked.

"Where the fuck is my money?" Law gripped Dash by the collar of his shirt and hemmed him against the wall.

"I don't know what the fuck you're talking about. What money?"

"Don't play fucking stupid with me. I know y'all robbed our fucking store. Where the fuck is the money?"

"What is he talking about, Dash?" Mrs. Hurts questioned.

"I—I don't know."

"Robbed the store when?" Honey proceeded to ask.

"Not too long ago," I answered. Law's nostrils flared as he eyeballed Dash.

"That's not possible. Dash has been here all day," Mrs. Hurts replied.

"And you're sure of that?"

"Yes. He's been helping me with a few things around here today. It's not possible that he could have robbed y'all."

Law released his grip on Dash, and he dropped to the floor. He didn't even apologize for whupping his ass before he stormed out of there.

CHAPTER FIFTEEN
DASH

Once the front door shut, Ma rushed over to me and roughly gripped me by the forearm. "Did you fucking do it?" she asked, not caring that Streets was still standing there.

"No. I swear I didn't. I don't know what he's talking about."

"Someone robbed the main building downtown today. Do you have any idea of Wick's whereabouts?" Streets questioned me, and I shook my head. "You think he's stupid enough to pull something off like that?"

"I don't know." I shrugged. "You'd probably have to find him and ask him that yourself."

"I'm gon' get to the bottom of it," were Streets' last words as he marched downstairs.

"Y'all really be having too much going on," Honey said. She'd been so quiet that I forgot she was even standing there. "Wick really gon' be the death of you. I seriously don't know why you be hanging with that bum in the first place." Shaking her head, she went back into her bedroom and shut the door behind her.

"I'm telling you now, if anything else comes back to this family that can hurt us because of your stupid actions, I'm going to kill you myself," Ma said and stormed off.

Whipping my phone from my pocket, I dialed Wick's number. The phone rang all the way to the voicemail. Slipping it back into my pocket, I went into the bathroom to clean my face before leaving the house. My lip split from Law's punch to the face. That nigga caught me off guard. Had I seen the shit coming, I would have fought his ass back. Nigga thought that just because he was a Blanco, everyone was supposed to fear him. I be trying to keep my cool on behalf of my family, but if he kept bullying me like that, we was gon' have a problem.

Exiting the house, I climbed into my car and headed for Wick's house to see if he was there. The nigga had yet to call me back to see what I wanted, and I needed to know if it was really him that robbed the Blancos. That man was really losing his fucking mind. If he had me steal a car filled with drugs from them, there was no doubt in my mind that he would go take their money. That was probably the insane ass idea he had the last time we spoke. Since I didn't go along with whatever he was concocting, he hadn't really been talking to me much lately.

Pulling up to Wick's house, I found his car parked outside. He was definitely in there. Question is, how come he hadn't called me back yet?

Getting out the car, I went up to the front door and knocked on it. The door pulled open and I was face to face with Faye, his mama. "Hey, baby. How you been doing?" she asked me and stepped to the side for me to enter the house.

"I'm good, Mrs. Peterman. Is Wick around? I saw his car out front."

"Yeah, he's back there in his room. I told him a thousand times to turn that fucking music down, but he don't want to listen. He gon' be out that door in a minute." She frowned.

"I'll see if I can talk to him."

"I don't know why he can't be sweet like you. Thanks, baby," she said and shut the door behind me.

I trotted back toward Wick's bedroom and heard Moneybagg Yo blasting. I understood where she was coming from. He had the music so fucking loud as if he was having a party in his bedroom. Knocking on the door, I stood back and waited for him to come to it. After standing there two minutes, I banged harder.

"Got damn, Ma! I told you I was—" His words caught in his throat when he pulled the door open and saw me standing there. "Wha-what are you doing here?" he asked, glancing over his shoulder and pulling the door closer to his frame. If he was trying to hide the cash lying all over his bed, he was doing a terrible job at it. I'd already seen it.

Pushing the door away from him, I asked, "Where'd you get the money?"

Wick yanked me into the bedroom and shut the door behind me. "Do you have to be so fucking loud?"

My eyes roamed the bed that was covered with so much cash, I couldn't even see the sheets. "Where the fuck did you get that shit from?" I asked him again, already knowing full and well where it came from. Law was gon' kill him.

This nigga looked me dead in my face and said, "You don't wanna know."

"You stole that shit from the Blancos, didn't you?"

"If you already knew where it came from, why the fuck you asking?" Wick picked up a handful of money and dropped it over my head. "Wait, how the hell you even know that?"

"You fucking dummy, they came to the house thinking I stole it."

"And what you told 'em?" he asked as he took a seat on the edge of the bed.

"That I don't know nothing 'bout no robbery."

"Good."

"The fuck you mean good? Nigga, I ain't have shit to do with that shit. I didn't even know you stole anything, but what's not gon' happen is this shit not 'bout to come back and bite me in the ass. You need to give that money back."

"Nigga, is you crazy?" Wick's brows snapped together. "I'm not 'bout to give shit back. You already fucked me when you gave that car back, this shit mine. Fuck outta here." He waved me off.

"Do you not know what them niggas will do to you if they found out that you stole they shit? What they'd do to your fucking family..."

He lifted to his feet and poked me hard in the chest with his index finger, then said, "They not gon' find out. Now are they?" His head cocked to the side and he awaited my response.

"What the fuck you gon' do with all that money anyway?"

"For starters, I'm gon' get my family out the hood. Nigga, we deserve a good life too."

"Do you really think you gon' get far taking shit from people?"

"I do what the fuck needs to be done. By any means." He bumped me hard by the shoulder, and I stumbled a bit. Stepping back, I stood there eyeing him as he went into the closet and grabbed a duffle. "But you wouldn't know none 'bout that. Would you?"

"You act like my life is all it's cracked up to be when it ain't. I'd kill to have a family like yours. I damn near begged my pops to be a father, and that nigga looked me dead in the eyes and told me that him providing this lifestyle for us should be enough. They fucking pawned Honey off to the Blancos like she's fucking property. You on the outside looking in and thinking shit sweet when it's not."

"Pssh, whatever," was the only response he could give me before reaching down and picking the money up from the floor. "You still got a good life. If I could trade places with you, I would."

"Take it, Wick!" Moisture filled my eyes. I really wish he knew what the hell he was asking for.

"Why you being so fucking dramatic?" Shaking his head, he continued to stuff all the cash into his duffel. "I'm out of here," he said once all the money was inside, and he zipped the bag.

"Where the hell you going?"

"None of your fucking business," were his last words as he sauntered out the bedroom.

CHAPTER SIXTEEN
HONEY
A COUPLE DAYS LATER

Ada had invited me out for lunch. Since I wasn't doing anything, I agreed to go. Unlike the others, she was sweet as hell. Why wouldn't I want to spend time with her? If I was stuck with this family, I might as well have someone that I can bond with.

The shit that happened the day before had been playing over in my mind. The way Law came into that house acting all reckless and shit. He didn't even bother to ask questions, just immediately placed his hands on Dash and didn't bother to apologize afterward when he found out he wasn't even the person to blame. It enraged me to know that I was about to be tied to this man for the rest of my life.

Shaking the thoughts from my mind, I stepped out of the walk-in closet with my sweater dress and slipped it on. After lunch, once Coco got out of class, I was gon' shoot her a couple ideas I had for our birthday trip. When I say I can't wait 'til we board that plane and get the fuck out of here, I can't fucking wait. I just wanted to put as much distance between me and Law as possible.

It was crazy how we were under the same roof and he made it his mission that we never saw each other. I ate every single meal in this house alone. It wasn't bad because I was enjoying the peace, but I didn't know if this was how I wanted the rest of my life to be. When Ada asked me to lunch, I jumped at the opportunity where I didn't have to eat alone.

Pulling my hair back into a ponytail at the nape of my neck, I applied my favorite Fenty lip gloss and grabbed my Birkin. By the time I made it out the door, the driver was already standing at the back door waiting for me. "I'm going to Golden Rosé," I told him and climbed into the back seat. He shut the door behind me and got into the driver's seat.

My phone began to ring as we pulled out the driveway and I saw it was Marcia calling. "Hey," I answered.

"Giiiiiiirl, the dress I ordered for your engagement party just came and it's fire as hell."

"Please don't remind me that bullshit is coming up." I rolled my eyes. I was far from ready to parade around a party and pretend like I was happy being there. If anyone asked me, I could do without all that shit. They should have let us just go on to the courthouse and call it a day. Shit, this felt like a prison sentence anyway. Life without possibility of parole.

"If I was in your shoes, I'd be jumping for joy."

"Why don't you marry his ass then?" My brow arched to my hairline.

"If I could, I would. He wants you though. Everyone knows I ain't a virgin."

"Technically, he doesn't want me. His daddy wanted me for him, but whatever."

"You don't have to be nasty about it. We all understand that you don't want to marry him." My eyes shifted to my ring. It had been tempting as fuck to just take it off. Everywhere I went, people noticed it and were congratulating me as if it was supposed to be some celebration.

"I'm on my way to meet Ada. I'll call you back later."

"Wait, who's—"

I disconnected the call before she was able to finish asking me her question. For the remainder of the ride to Golden Rosé, it was silent. When we got there, Ada was already inside. I was running a bit behind. The driver opened the door for me, and I went inside.

"How many?" the hostess stopped me at the door and asked.

"I'm meeting someone here. They're already inside."

Stepping around her, my eyes roamed the building in search of Ada and they didn't have to go far because they landed straight on her. She sat at one of the tables by the window with a glass of wine in front of her. Ada could have easily already ordered her food but judging by how the menu was still in front of her, she'd been waiting on me to get here.

Nearing the table, I stopped and said, "Hey." A smile plastered on her face. She lifted to her feet and gripped me by the hands before planting a kiss on my cheek. Ada was small and fragile. She was so tiny compared to me.

"You look beautiful as always," Ada complimented and took her seat.

"Thank you."

I sat down at the table directly in front of her and picked up the menu, going straight to the drinks section. The way life had been set up lately, I needed liquor but knew I wasn't quite old enough to order it just yet. Lifting my hand in the air, I called the waitress over and ordered a Sprite.

"Do you need a little time to look over the menu?"

"Yes, please," I told her.

"I'll be right back with your drink." She bounced away from the table and I took my attention back to the menu. This restaurant was Ada's choice. I hadn't really eaten here often and didn't really know what to order.

"Are you ready for your engagement party?" Ada asked, in hopes to break the ice. My eyes cut in her direction, and she snickered. "I know this situation isn't really ideal for you, but you're probably going to be the best thing that ever happened to Law. Just wait and see. I can feel it in my bones." She offered me a smile.

"I don't know about all that."

"Did you at least pick out a dress for it yet?"

"Not really."

"When do you plan on doing it? Do you want me to do it for you?"

I quickly shook my head. I had nothing against Ada, but I wasn't about to wear anything that she picked out. "I'll find something soon."

The waitress came back with my drink and took our orders. As we sat there at the table waiting for our food to come back, we engaged in small talk. "How come someone had to be chosen for Law to marry?" If I was stuck with this man for the rest of my life, it did no harm in learning a few things about him.

"Baby, Lawrence doesn't want to be in a relationship let alone marry anyone. He's supposed to take over the family business and, in this family, for a man to take over, he has to be married. There's no ifs, ands, or buts about it. Trust me, Law has tried everything in his power not to suffer this fate and that's the exact reason why his father took matters into his own hands."

"How come he doesn't want to be in a relationship?"

"A few years ago, Law's mother got killed. A rival family murdered her. He sat there and witnessed the pain it put his father through, and he didn't want to experience anything like it, so he swore off commitment with women."

"I'm so sorry to hear that."

"I tried to tell him that he can't go throughout life like that. A man needs a woman, and a woman needs a man. Being in love can be one of the most beautiful things ever."

"Have you ever been in love before?" I asked her and took a sip of my Sprite from the straw. A woman bumped my arm, and I jerked forward, almost spilling my drink.

"I'm so sorry," she quickly made known. "Caleb, slow down!" she shouted behind her toddler. "Did it waste? Do you need napkins or something?" She nervously chuckled. "Kids really are the devil."

"It's fine." I zeroed in on the little boy that was zooming a toy plane through the air as he ran around the restaurant. It took my mind back to the fact that I was gon' have to have sexual intercourse with Law and make a mini monster of my own. Kids had never been on my radar. Hell, I wasn't even certain if I'd make a good mother. I thought I had plenty of time to decide if I wanted to navigate through life with kids, and now I'm told that I have a year of freedom before I'm to become a mother. It's not fair. A woman should be able to decide if she wants to put her body through that trauma. Some of the women don't even survive in those rooms and they wanted me to put my life on the line for a man that I don't love, barely even know, and don't even know if I'd ever like him.

Snapping from my thoughts, I took my attention back to Ada. She beamed me a smile. "What?" I questioned her.

"You're worried about having kids, aren't you?"

"I don't even know if I'm ready for kids right now and I

have to agree to produce one within the first year. That's a lil bizarre, isn't it?"

Ada snickered. "You're young. I get that. But once you have a child, you'll be just fine. Those motherly instincts will come right out of you. When I first got married to Herbert, God rest his soul, I was overwhelmed. I had to go through something similar. I wasn't in love with him at first, but once I got to know him, the love came. That man turned out to be my soulmate and I couldn't imagine life without him."

"That's amazing, but that doesn't mean that Law and I will have the same fate. That man wants nothing to do with me. I haven't spent any time with him. He forces me to eat every single meal alone. It's lonely there."

"Sounds like to me, he's trying to push you away. You just have to push back," she said as the waitress placed our plates down on the table in front of us.

For the remainder of lunch, we had small talk, just getting to know each other better. Once lunch was over, we hugged and went our separate ways. I ended up going back to the house. As expected, Law wasn't there.

I ended up wandering on his wing of the house to see what all the fuss was about me staying from over there. Nigel made it certain that I knew I wasn't allowed in his bedroom, and I wanted to know why. Before I headed in that direction, I peeped and saw that Nigel had fallen asleep in the chair in the kitchen.

Stopping at the first door, I pulled on the knob, and it wouldn't open. "Hhmm," I said and strolled off to the next room. I found a bedroom but it wasn't big enough to be considered Law's. My bedroom was bigger than this one. Shutting the door, I moved on to the next room. After opening a good five doors, I finally found what I assumed was his room. It was black. Like everything was literally black. He didn't have a splash of color in that bedroom whatsoever. It was kind of depressing actually.

I wandered into his bedroom and opened his walk-in closet. All his clothes were color coordinated. Nothing seemed out of place. Even his accessories were coordinated as well. I stopped at his cologne and took a whiff of the Dior one. Placing it back on the shelf, I noticed a door at the back of his closet. Thinking it led to his bathroom, I turned the knob and my heart dropped to my ass.

"What the fuck?" I whispered as if someone was gon' hear me.

Before me was yet another bedroom, but this one had a black and red canopy bed in there. On the wall next to it was all sorts of whips, chains, and cuffs. All types of shit to torture someone with. Red LED lights lined the floorboards and ceiling. I stepped further into the room, heart palpitating as I neared a dresser and opened the drawer. The first drawer was filled with lingerie. The second one had all different types of sex toys.

"What the fuck?" I whispered.

"I'll grab it for you, sir," I heard Nigel's voice and shut the drawer. Rushing out the room, I closed the door behind me and hid in the closet, praying that he didn't come in there and find me. My heart pound against my ribcage as I waited for Nigel to do whatever he needed to so I could get the hell out of there.

My heart dropped to my feet when Nigel stopped directly in front of me with his phone up to his ear. "Yes, sir, I'm still here. I found it," he said and stepped around me, grabbing a coat off a hanger. "I'll send it right over," he told him and ended the call. "What are you doing here?"

"How come you didn't rat me out?"

"I like you. If Mr. Blanco found out you were in his bedroom, he'd be angry." Roughly gripping me by the forearm, he pulled me out the room and continued. "Stay out of his room, please." After finding that extra room in his closet, I figured that was the reason he didn't want me in there.

"Okay," I said and stood there, watching Nigel as he trotted down the hallway toward the staircase.

CHAPTER SEVENTEEN
LAW

My truck pulled into the driveway and the house was pitch black. That's normally how it looked when I made it home. It's been my mission not to come to this house 'til at least one or two in the morning. From what I've observed, Honey wasn't the type to stay up late. At least three days out the week, she had class the next day and was up and out the house before nine.

The truck stopped and Fredrick opened the door for me. "You can head home. I'm not going anywhere else tonight. I'll see you in the morning," I told him, and he nodded. I entered the house and went straight for the kitchen where I knew there was a plate waiting for me in the microwave. That had become my daily routine, coming in late and enjoying dinner alone.

Placing my keys on the counter, I opened the microwave and pulled the top off the container. Shutting the door, I turned the microwave on and poured myself a glass of D'USSÉ on the rocks. The microwave beeped and my eyes darted in the direction of the doorway as if Honey was gon' be able to hear that shit all the way upstairs. Grabbing the plate, I made myself comfortable on the barstool. My phone chimed with an email alert. Opening the folder, I saw that it was from the photographer. Our engagement pictures had come back. Biting the bullet, I opened 'em just to see how they turned out, and from what I could see, people wouldn't even know that we couldn't stand each other's guts. Old dude did a great job on the photos.

I jumped at the sound of Honey clearing her throat from behind me. "For someone to be a ruthless killer, you're damn sure jumpy. Scary ass," she said and rounded the island. Hitting the power button on my phone, I turned my attention back to my salmon that was getting cold. "So you do eat dinner. Just not with me, huh?" Getting on her tippy toes, she reached for a glass in the cabinet. Her frame leaned into the counter and my eyes danced over her frame. Her ass cheeks were playing peek-a-boo in the silk pink pajama shorts she wore. Finally grabbing the glass, she took her bougie ass over to the fridge and grabbed a bottle of water then poured it into it.

"Why not just drink from the fucking bottle?"

"Oh damn, you can talk." She rolled her eyes and turned her cup up. "It's crazy that you'd rather starve yourself 'til the wee hours of the night instead of being civil and sitting down to eat dinner with me." Her glass clacked against the counter, and she folded her arms over her chest as if that was supposed to force me to answer her. I focused on my dinner, avoiding her question. "You act like I'm such a terrible person to be around. We're both stuck in this shit. We might as well make the most of it."

"Why are you still talking to me?"

"I truly get it. No one in their right mind will marry you. I don't care how much money you got. You're rude, evil, and only God knows what else. Your mama was probably glad when she died. She didn't have to deal with you no more." My hand tightly gripped my fork and my gaze shot to hers.

"I suggest you get the fuck out of here before I do something you'll regret."

"Fuck you."

Honey rounded the island to leave, and I went back to my meal. That bullshit she just said 'bout my mama was uncalled for. She was lucky she was still breathing in this mufucka. No one got to speak on my mama and lived to tell 'bout that shit. The way she was taken from us was so tragic. She really didn't deserve that shit. It was one of the reasons why I was so cold toward people, unless we were doing business that is.

To get the phone call that your mama was gun downed and left for dead inside her car was a hard pill to swallow when you were a child. That shit stuck with me for life. Sometimes, it was all I could think about. Pops took her death so hard. He never moved on. There wasn't a time I could name that I saw him with another woman or heard anything about it. He couldn't sleep or eat for days. To this day, he still blames himself for her death and took it even harder 'cause he was never able to find out who truly pulled the trigger on her. So much blood was shed, and no one was talking. Mama Ada finally was able to talk him down off the ledge.

I was pulled from my thoughts when I felt something sharp pressed against my throat. Lavender clouded my head, and I instantly knew who was stupid enough to do some bullshit like this.

"Honey, you might as well gon' cut my throat at this point," I warned her.

"I don't want this fucking life," she damn near choked on her words. Tears dampened my shoulder. "I can't spend the rest of my life being attached to you." My heart stung to know that she'd rather kill me than spend one more second around me. "Why couldn't y'all just let me go?"

In one swift motion, I gripped her wrist and pressed my thumb in between the bones in it. "Ahh!" she screamed out and her grip on the knife loosened. Before she knew it, she was bear hugged from behind with the very knife she was threatening to take my life with firmly against her throat.

"You know, it really didn't have to come down to this."

"I'm still young. Y'all want me to throw away my life to become your wife. Y'all want me to have yo' kids and you can't even stand to be in the same room with me," she said in between sobs. "I never asked for this shit."

Technically, you did. We asked for Coco.

But she was right. She didn't ask for any of this shit. I kinda somewhat understood where she was coming from and that was the exact reason why she wasn't bleeding on my kitchen floor right now.

Dropping the knife to the floor, I slung her over my shoulder and carried her to her bedroom where she was gon' stay 'til I felt like releasing her. Whenever that's gon' be. I tossed her against her bed and said, "Yo' ass will stay in this fucking room 'til I feel like letting you out. The only place you're allowed to go is school and back here."

"What!" Her eyes bucked and she bounced to her feet.

"You'll have plenty time to think 'bout the shit you just pulled."

"You're joking, right?" she questioned me. Tears filled the brims of her eyes.

"I'm not one to joke or play games."

"But I have a birthday trip coming up."

"You should have thought 'bout that shit before you tried to kill me. You're lucky this the only punishment you're getting. Be thankful that you're still breathing," I told her and turned for the door.

"Law, you can't lock me in here! I'm not a fucking child!" she screamed at my back.

Without speaking another word, I grabbed the doorknob. Honey made a dash in my direction, but the door was closed and locked before she could reach it.

"Law! Let me out of here!" she yelled and banged on the door. "Law!"

"Every action got consequences," I said and strolled away from the door.

CHAPTER EIGHTEEN
COCO
A COUPLE DAYS LATER

"Answer the phone," I said out loud as I paced my bedroom floor. This was the third time I'd called Honey today and she wasn't answering the phone. When the phone rolled over to voicemail, I slipped it into my back pocket and said, "Alright, I'm coming over," and exited my bedroom. Honey knew how I got whenever she went without talking to me. I knew she was fine because we had these twin instincts. We could always tell when something was wrong with the other.

"Take me to Honey," I told my driver when I made it outside. Nodding, he opened the back door for me, and I climbed into the seat.

It didn't take us long to make it to Honey's new home. The driver opened the door for me and I went up and knocked on the front door. I nibbled on my thumbnail waiting for someone to answer it. The door pulled open and this older gentleman stood there. From his white gloves, I sensed he was the help.

"Hey, I'm looking for Honey. Is she here?"

His lips parted to speak, but he was interrupted by Ada's

voice. "It's okay, Nigel, I got it," she said and tapped him on the forearm. Nodding, he strolled off.

"Hey, Coco. What are you doing here?"

"I was looking for Honey. Have you seen her?"

"Honey is a lil tied up right now. I'm actually glad that you're here. She was supposed to go sample the cakes today but can't make it. Do you mind going in her place? You know her better than I do. I'm sure you'd know what type of cake she'd want."

"You sure we shouldn't just wait 'til she's able to go?"

"I'll write down the address for you. I'd hate for us to get behind schedule for the wedding. I asked Law if he'd go, but he's not really the sweets type of person and he doesn't know much about Honey to choose the right flavor for her."

She stepped away from the door and opened the drawer on the table in the foyer. Ada grabbed a piece of paper and pen and jotted down the address to the bakery and handed it to me.

"You're a huge help. Thanks, Coco," she said as if I already agreed to go.

"Sure," I replied and turned away from the door. I gazed down at the piece of paper and couldn't help but wonder exactly what had Honey so busy that she couldn't answer the phone for me.

I went back to the truck and handed the driver the paper. "Take me to this address," I told him and relaxed back against the seat. As we rode to the bakery, I went onto Honey's Facebook and saw that she hadn't posted anything in a couple days. That was strange to me seeing how she was always on social media. If I didn't hear anything back from her, I was gon' break in that house and find my damn sister.

We pulled into the parking lot of Fancy Cakez. I got out the truck and went inside. There were a couple other people in there at the counter picking out what they wanted out the glass. I stood back and waited 'til they were done so I could speak with someone. Ada didn't really give me any instructions. All she said was come try some samples for Honey. The door dinged and I turned around and saw Streets standing there.

"What are you doing here?" I questioned him.

"I could ask you the same thing but seems like we've been set up."

"She asked you to come too, huh?"

Chuckling, he replied, "Yeah."

"So it's not enough that y'all have Honey, she's trying to pawn me off too."

"I wouldn't look at it like that. She just thinks that she's doing what's best."

"Next!" the woman behind the counter called out, grasping both of our attention.

Streets and I both moved toward the counter. "Hi. We were sent here to do some cake tasting for the Blanco wedding."

A huge smile adorned her face. She covered her mouth with her hands and bounced on her tippy toes. "Are you the bride and groom?"

My face turned beet red. "Oh no. I'm not getting married. I'm the maid of honor and he's the best man," I corrected her.

"I'm so excited and thrilled that they trusted me to do their cake. This is the biggest wedding I've ever done. You can have a seat. I'll bring some samples out to you."

Streets and I made our way over to one of the tables by the window and sat down. "Why you had to answer her like that back there?" he questioned me.

"What do you mean?"

"You answered like it'd be something terrible to be getting married to me."

A nervous giggle escaped my lips. "Oh, no. I promise it was nothing like that. I hardly know you. How could it be?"

The woman brought a tray of tiny cakes over to our table. "Just let me know what flavor and frosting you like. I'll be right over there if you need me," she said and bounced away from the table.

"I'm trying to understand what you're tasing cake for when Ada told me that Law doesn't really do sweets."

"Maybe she just wanted a second opinion. Either way, it's for the wedding and whatever Mama Ada wants, she always manages to get."

Grabbing a fork, he dug into the double chocolate cake with chocolate frosting. It was a lil too much chocolate for me, which I already knew Honey wasn't gon' be feeling.

"Why are you looking at me like that?" he asked as he brought the fork up to his lips.

"You don't think that's too much chocolate? I mean, I'm a chocolate girl, but I can't do that much. Makes my teeth hurt just from looking at it." I watched him as his eyes shut and he chewed the cake. From his facial expression, I sensed the cake was good, but I still passed on it.

"It's actually pretty good. You should give it a try." I quickly shook my head and scanned the tray for the piece of cake I wanted to try. "Seriously, try it." He brought his fork toward my face. Our gazes lingered for a moment. His dark eyes pulled me in, and I knew he wasn't gon' stop bugging me about this cake.

Opening my mouth, he placed his fork inside. I moaned when I tasted the chocolate. "See, what I tell you?" The corner of his mouth quirked.

"It's good. I give you that, but it's not Honey's taste. We're here to get something that she'd love, remember?"

"Which one do you think she'd like?"

"Honey is a plain girl. She'd probably want a vanilla cake and maybe some whipped frosting. It don't take much to make her happy."

"And what makes you happy?"

My eyes shot in Streets' direction. He'd caught me off guard with that question. No one had really asked me what makes me happy. I just typically went along with anything they wanted. I was somewhat a people pleaser. That's exactly how I got dragged into a lot of shit I wasn't up for doing.

"Seeing everyone around me happy. Oh, and books. Lots and lots of books."

"So you like to read?"

"Like is an understatement. I love reading. I'm actually reading a book on my Kindle now and it's so good."

"Really?" Streets' undivided attention rotated to me. "What's it about?"

"It's about this baseball player that falls for this publicist. Oh my God, I just love them together. I'm on the part where he's about to find out that she's been keeping this secret from him. I know he's gon' be upset, but I really hope he don't end up breaking her heart."

"You sound really invested."

"I'm sorry, I just get carried away when it comes to books." I picked at a piece of red velvet cake with my fork.

"You don't have to be sorry. I like hearing you talk."

My cheeks burned and I brought my gaze back to his. "Streets, can I ask you something?"

"Wassup?" he asked and stuffed a piece of cake into his mouth.

"How come you're single? You seem like a really nice guy. Why hasn't any woman snatched you up yet?"

"Honestly, I haven't really been looking. I'm not in a rush for no fake love. That seems to be the only thing that's out here nowadays. The shit my parents had is gone. People don't believe in true love anymore. All they wanna do is use the other person."

"I definitely understand that."

"You got a great head on your shoulders and you're beautiful as fuck. Why nobody bagged you yet?"

"When people find out that I'm a virgin, they tend to laugh. At my big ass age, I haven't had sex yet. Some men find out and bedding me becomes their full goal. I guess what I'm saying is, I'm just like you. I'm not in a rush for fake love." I let off a shrug.

Streets' eyes danced over my face. This was the longest he'd ever held my gaze. "Well, I think it's brave of you to still be holding on to your virginity. A lot of girls your age are bouncing from dick to dick. Hell, some of 'em got more mileage on 'em than a box Chevy. You need to give that shit to someone who deserves it. Whatever nigga comes along, just make sure he works for it, a'ight?"

Before I could answer him, we were interrupted by the owner. "How's everything going over here?" she asked with her hand resting on her hip. "Do you need anything?"

"I think I've decided on a cake. I'm going to go with the vanilla with butter cream frosting."

"That sounds like a good choice. Did they say what sort of theme they were going for yet?"

"Not that I know of, but I'm sure they'll let you know once they find out. Do you mind if I take some of this cake to go?"

"Sure, I don't mind." She grabbed the tray off the table and went back behind the counter. Streets looked down at his phone and lifted to his feet. I kinda hated that the short time we spent together was coming to an end. The woman came back with a box and handed it to me. "It was a pleasure working with you. Maybe we can do this again sometime in the future."

"I'll definitely keep you in mind," I told her and rose to my feet. "Thank you."

Streets walked me out the door to my truck. We stopped, and I faced him. "Even though I didn't really want to do this, I had a good time."

"I'm glad you did. Maybe we can do this again sometime." The corner of my mouth quirked. "I mean something else. Not cake tasting."

"Would you be asking me on a date, Streets?"

"I don't know. Would you want to go on a date with me?"

"Wouldn't that be strange? Your brother is marrying my sister."

"What that have to do with me?"

"I'd have to think on it."

"Take all the time you need. I'm in no rush." His lips brushed the corner of my mouth, and my body went rigid. "Have a nice rest of the day," he said and opened the door for me. He shut it once I was secured in the vehicle.

CHAPTER NINETEEN
STREETS
LATER THAT DAY

We were out a good hundred thousand dollars because of the robbery. We had been trying our best to find out exactly who the hell did it. Law had his assumptions: Wick. For now we weren't certain, but if I were Wick, I'd go into hiding. Law wasn't stopping 'til he got to the bottom of it.

Since the robbery, I had been trying to figure out ways to keep my employees safe. We were too comfortable, and it was time to turn shit up a notch. Though they were behind bulletproof glass, they were still touchable. I'd placed men at all the locations off the strength that I didn't know if this was a one-time thing or not. The last thing I wanted to happen was they hit another building and we be out even more cash. Though we had three other locations, none of 'em housed as much cash as the downtown location.

As I sat in my office and went over the surveillance for what seemed like the millionth time, I tried to spot anything that could help me identify the mufuckas that robbed us. A knock at my office door grasped my attention. "Yeah?"

The door pushed in and Charlene stood there. "There's some guy up front wanting to speak with you. Says it's important."

"Did he say what it was about?" She shook her head. "A'ight, I'm coming." Charlene shut the door and I powered my computer down. Despite anyone not supposed to be back here, I never left out of any office without turning the computer off.

Getting up from my desk, I went up front to see who was looking for me. Imagine my surprise when I bent the corner and saw Dash standing there. "You haven't gotten enough showing up places you're unwanted?" I asked him, and he jumped at the sound of my voice.

"Technically, our last altercation, I was at home. Can I speak to you in private?" He glanced back over his shoulder out the glass window and my eyes darted in that direction, but I didn't see anything.

"I guess. C'mon." I led him down the hallway to my office and shut the door behind us. "What do you want?" I wasted no time asking him.

"I wanted to talk to you 'bout the robbery."

"Thought you didn't know shit 'bout it?" My brow arched to my hairline.

"I didn't, but if I tell you this, you have to promise that he won't know it came from me."

"Who?"

"Just promise that you'll keep me confidential before I say anything."

"A'ight. Hurry up and get to it. I do have other things to do."

"Wick robbed y'all."

"And you're sure? How do you know?"

"He told me himself. I even saw the money."

"How come you're telling me? Isn't he supposed to be your best friend?"

"Yeah, but when that friend keeps making decisions that could put me and my family in danger, I have to speak the fuck up. He's getting outrageous and won't listen to anyone."

"You do know what that means, right? That he's gon' have to be put down."

"I understand that. It's either him or my family, and I can't let anything else happen to them."

"Smart man." Rounding my desk, I took a seat in my chair and told him, "You can get the fuck out now."

Nodding, Dash exited my office and shut the door behind him. I sat there, relaxed back in my chair, pondering if I was 'bout to tell Law now 'bout the shit that was just brought to me or if I was gon' wait. His engagement party was tomorrow. He probably had his hands full with that. Maybe I'd wait 'til afterward before I said something.

I went by the house to check on Mama A. Since Honey had been missing in action, she had the weight of planning the engagement party on her and the wedding planner. Mama A didn't too much mind. She was excited to know that Law was finally 'bout to marry and produce her a great-grandbaby. That's all she ever spoke about, wanting to see her great-grandbabies before she died.

When I entered the house, I found Mama A in the kitchen. She was making one of her famous turkey sandwiches. "Hey, Ma." I went over and pecked her softly on the cheek. "You making that for me?"

She beamed a smile up at me.

"I didn't even know you were coming by here today."

"I just stopped by to check on you for a second. I wanted to see how everything is going for tomorrow."

"Everything is fine," she said and went over to the refrigerator and grabbed a personal bottle of cranberry juice.

"Now, I know you're not 'bout to eat that. Who's that for?"

"I was making my granddaughter-in-law some lunch if that's fine with you."

"What's going on with her anyway?"

Mama A shrugged. "I don't know. Law said he put her in her bedroom, and she is to stay in there 'til tomorrow night. I don't know what happened, but I'm not 'bout to let her starve up there. She hasn't been eating anything. Every plate Nigel puts at her door, she doesn't touch. I figured maybe she'd eat this."

"Let me take it up there to her." I only offered to see what the hell was going on. Law had her ass in that room like she was a grounded teen.

"That's sweet of you. Try to get her to at least take a bite."

"I'll see what I can do." Taking the tray from her, I went upstairs to Honey's bedroom and knocked on the door. I went to turn the knob and noticed it was locked but from the outside. Opening the door, I found Honey laying in the center of her bed, staring up at the ceiling.

"Nigel, I told you that I'm not hungry," she said, not even looking in my direction.

"It's me."

Honey shot straight up in bed and eyeballed me. "What do you want?"

"I came to see what's going on. Why you locked in here?"

"Why don't you ask your brother that," she said, pouting, folding her arms over her chest.

"What the hell did you do?" I questioned her and set the tray on the nightstand.

"What makes you think I did something?"

"Law don't have yo' ass locked in this room for no reason."

"Fine. I tried to kill him."

"And you're still breathing?" I stroked my chin. "That's a first."

"Can you blame me though? You're brother isn't really the nicest person." I chuckled. *That's true.* "Now he won't let me out this fucking room. Can you talk to him or something? I have a birthday trip coming up and he's not even gon' let me go."

"I don't know what me talking to him gon' solve. Law's stubborn as shit. Once he makes his mind up, that's it."

"Sitting in this room is driving me fucking insane. He even took my fucking phone. I try to take extra time when I go to class so that I won't get back here so soon, but those stupid ass drivers of his won't even take me anywhere else. I fucking hate it here." She crashed back against the bed.

"I know you might not like how he's treating you right now..." Honey's head snapped in my direction. "Just be thankful that you're still alive. He could have killed you for trying to kill him. Mama A fixed you something to eat. She's worried 'bout you up here. Just take a bite so she knows you aren't starving yourself to death."

"Whatever." Honey turned over and gave me her back.

"From what I can tell, you and him are more alike than you think," were my last words as I exited the room and locked the door back.

CHAPTER TWENTY
HONEY
THE ENGAGEMENT PARTY

For the last hour, I had been sitting here staring at that dress bag. I'd taken my shower, got my hair and makeup done, but I'd yet to put my dress on. People were waiting for me to arrive. I was supposed to have shown up at the party over forty minutes ago. Since I'd been confined to this room, one would think I'd jump at the opportunity to be out there in civilization, but something about that party just wasn't sitting right with me. How could I go and pretend to be happy when I was anything but?

Law had been treating me like a scorned child. Honestly, I couldn't even blame him, but he was taking shit too fucking far. I hadn't laid eyes on him ever since he placed me in this room, and I wasn't sure how things were gon' play out when I saw him tonight. My heart banged against my ribcage from the knock at my bedroom door.

"Ms. Honey, are you ready? Everyone is waiting for you," Nigel said from the opposite side.

"Just five minutes," I replied and straightened my posture. Unzipping the dress bag, I pulled out the gold, satin, off-shoulder, mermaid, long split, beaded gown. It was gorgeous as hell. This was the first time I'd seen it. Mama A picked it out for me since I couldn't really go anywhere. I was terrified that she'd pick up something I wouldn't want to wear.

Slipping the dress on, I stepped into the floor-length mirror to look at my reflection and I was blown away. From my head down to my feet, I was stunning. Too bad all this was going to waste on a mufucka that didn't even deserve me.

Grabbing my clutch off the dresser, I exited the bedroom, bumping right into Nigel. "Ms. Honey, you look breathtaking."

"Thank you. Let's get this bullshit over with." Nigel led me to the staircase where my driver waited for me downstairs at the front door. The engagement party was being hosted in the ballroom at the Millionaire Suites downtown. I climbed into the truck and silently rode all the way to the hotel.

When we arrived, there were so many fucking cars in the parking lot and a red carpet that led up to the entrance. Paparazzi were all over the place. I should have known they'd pop up here once they got word that the governor's daughter was marrying into the wealthiest family in the city.

The driver stopped and opened the door for me. Soon as my foot touched the carpet, the lights began to flash in my eyes. I posed for a few pictures then entered the building. The first thing I saw was a sign with me and Law's name on it pointing in the direction of the ballroom. Covering the walls on the way to the door were different photos of me and Law separate and together. The engagement pictures came out beautiful. Prettier than I ever could've imagined. Despite the way I felt about him, we looked good together. We seemed like a couple in love, especially the photo of when we kissed.

I stopped in front of the ballroom door where two buff men stood. They were holding weapons, alerting me they were the security detail. One of them opened the door for me and I stepped inside. There were several people all over the room, laughing, talking, and drinking.

There was a huge black and gold balloon arch in front of the three-sixty photobooth with *Congratulations Honey and Law*. Clear balloons covered the ceiling with string lights inside of them looking as if we were staring up at the stars. Whoever decorated this really did their big one.

"There you are!" I turned and Ma was standing there with her arms stretched in my direction. "You had me thinking you weren't going to show up."

"I thought about it."

"If you hadn't, you know your father would have gone looking for you."

I rolled my eyes. He still wasn't my favorite person right now.

"Where's Coco?" I asked her as my eyes scanned the building in search of my sister. Other than school, this was gon' be my first time hanging out with her since Law's so-called punishment.

"She's around here somewhere with Marcia. I saw her not too long ago."

"Let me see if I can find her."

"You aren't going to go over there and speak to your fiancé?" My eyes landed on Law who stood there talking with Streets and some other people. He was dressed in a custom-tailored black suit with a gold shirt. That man was so fucking handsome for him to not have a soul.

"I'll pass," I said and walked off before she tried to force me to be cordial.

I maneuvered through the crowd 'til I found Coco and Marcia sitting at a table. Marcia had a glass up to her lips as Coco scrolled on her phone with her head resting in her hand. She looked as if she'd rather be anywhere else but here. Marcia was already twenty-one, that's why she was drinking and no one had anything to say about it. Ma let us drink wine but nothing stronger than that 'til we turned twenty-one. That's the exact reason why I used to sneak and drink.

"Y'all look bored."

Coco's eyes lifted to mine. "We bet you weren't coming."

"Ma said the same thing." I took the empty chair next to them at the table.

"This 'bout my third glass of champagne. Law and Streets know they look good tonight. Maybe I should try to see what Streets' dick is talking 'bout."

Coco cut her eyes at Marcia. I wasn't certain what all of that was about unless she had a thing for Streets and didn't tell me about it.

"Oh, my bad, girl. I almost forgot that you're the one who wanna fuck Streets."

"Shut up." Coco playfully pushed Marcia and she almost fell out of the chair.

"Wait, so you like Streets?" I asked her. This was my first time hearing of it.

Coco sat up straight in her chair and fiddled with her fingers, avoiding eye contact. "I don't know."

"What's wrong with liking him? He's much better than Law. If you like him, I say go for it."

"Baby, they are looking for you at the photobooth," Ma said, grabbing my attention.

Glancing up at her, I asked, "For what?"

"They want you and Law to take pictures."

Smacking my teeth, I rose to my feet and said, "Didn't we take enough for the engagement photos?"

"Honey, will you stop being so stubborn and just take the pictures?" Ma gripped me by the forearm and pulled me over to the photobooth where Law was standing there with his back facing me. "Here she is," Ma said, and Law turned around. His dark eyes bored into mine. This man smelled so fucking good, reminding me of the cologne I smelled in his closet.

His hand extended in my direction. I chewed on the inside of my jaw and rested mine in his. He helped me up onto the three-sixty photobooth and stepped alongside me.

"Oh my God, y'all look so good together. I don't know how many times I can say this," Mama Ada said as she stopped in front of us.

"You ready?" this woman asked as she stood in front of an iPad. I nodded and prepared to put on a show for everyone. The last thing I wanted was my face to be plastered all over the place in a scandal.

Law and I took several pictures together. My body melted into his frame.

"You two really be making magic together," Mama Ada made known.

Law released me and helped me back down to the floor. We went our separate ways for the remainder of the night 'til it was time for us to sit down and eat.

When eleven o'clock neared, everyone prepared to leave. I was stuck at Law's side because he instructed my driver to leave for the night and that I'd ride back to the house with him, which I thought was strange.

Law walked me out the door and opened the door on his truck for me. I climbed inside with him directly behind me. We rode home in silence. I kept glancing over at him as he looked down at his phone. The question that had been circling my brain slipped from my lips before I knew it. "What's up with that room I found in your closet?"

His eyes shot in my direction. "What the fuck were you doing in my room?"

"Can you blame me for being curious? Me being told not to

go in your room is like taking a horse to water and telling it not to drink from it. Can you explain that room to me? I've never seen anything like it."

"That's none of your fucking business," he simply answered and took his attention back to his phone.

"I'm about to be your wife. I think that is my business." Law ignored me, so I snatched his phone from his clutches. "I'm really tired of the way you be treating me. We're stuck with each other for the rest of our fucking lives. I refuse to live in silence whenever I'm around you. I found something and I want answers."

Law yanked his phone back from me and slipped it into his pocket. "I don't have to answer you. That's none of your fucking business," was all he said before he climbed out the truck and trotted into the house.

CHAPTER TWENTY-ONE
LAW
THE FOLLOWING DAY

"Are you really about to go through with this wedding?"

Tossing the covers back, I climbed out of bed, ignoring the fuck out of her question. That had been a question that I'd asked myself several times, especially after Honey tried to slice my throat. God had to have had his hands on me that day because she was supposed to be six feet under.

"Law, so you're really gon' act like you don't hear me talking to you?" She bolted from me, her breasts bouncing with every step she took in my direction.

"What's up with all you bitches being in my business lately? What I do is my fucking business."

"When you marry her, what's that gon' mean for us?"

"There's no fucking us. We fuck from time to time, I toss you some cash and we go our separate ways."

"So all I am is a quick nut to you?"

"What the fuck did you think it was?"

"Are you serious? We've been fucking for months. You can

honestly look me in my face and tell me that you don't feel nothing for me?"

Looking her dead in the face, I said, "I don't feel nothing for no one."

"How can you be so cold?"

Picking my clothes up from the floor, I reached into my pocket and pulled out a stack of cash then tossed it on the bed. "Pay yo' tuition for next semester or something," I said and proceeded to put my clothes on.

The stack smacked me in the face, and I mugged her. "Fuck you, Law. Your ass full of shit."

"You wanna be disrespectful, I'll take my shit back with me," I told her and picked it up from the floor. Shoving the money into my pocket, I grabbed my shirt and slipped it back on.

"You just disrespected me with the words that just left your lips. Your ass in here treating me like I'm a fucking ho." Marcia folded her arms over her chest and frowned. "You can marry a mufucka you don't even know but treat me like shit."

"Isn't that same mufucka yo' best friend?" My head cocked as I glowered at her. "You're the one to talk but still fucking me after you found out that we're engaged. What type of loyalty is that?"

"Loyalty?" Marcia snickered. "Nigga, you're her nigga and fucking me! The fuck you talking about! Yo' ass ain't loyal either!" Saliva sprayed from her lips. "Don't be standing in here tryna pretend like you're better than me."

"You're right. I need to stop fucking you. Anything else?"

Her mouth dropped to the floor. "That's not what I was saying."

"What the hell are you saying then?"

"Why her? If you're being forced to be married, how come you didn't choose me? At least you know that you'll be getting pussy whenever you want. Honey doesn't know the first thing 'bout sucking no dick let alone riding it."

"She can always be taught. You're acting like she isn't capable of learning. Plus, look how you're doing her, and she's supposed to be your best friend. I can only imagine what you'd do to me." My phone chimed and I looked down seeing it was a text from Streets.

Streets: *Wya? There's some I need to talk to you 'bout.*

Me: *Leaving the south. Hit my line in two minutes.*

"Law?" Marcia called out after me as I trotted out her room.

"I ain't got time for this shit, Marcia. I'm out."

Soon as I exited the house, my phone was ringing. "Yeah?" I answered and neared my truck.

"Law!" Marcia called my name again. I climbed into the truck and shut the door behind me, giving Streets my undivided attention.

"How fast can you make it downtown? What I need to talk to you 'bout can't be said over the phone."

"I'm on my way now," I told him and disconnected the call. "Take me to Blanco downtown," I instructed the driver.

When we arrived at the building, Streets' truck was the only one in the parking lot, which was understandable since it was after closing. Getting out the truck, I entered the building and found him in his office behind his desk with a cigar hanging from his lips. He picked up the box and offered me one, but I politely said, "I'm good." I wasn't there to smoke and be friendly. He called me here and I wanted to know why.

"Dash came to me with some information. He told me that Wick was the one who robbed us."

"You telling me some shit that I already know. He's the only person that's stupid enough to pull some bullshit like that."

"No, you had a feeling he did it and now you know for sure."

I clenched my teeth. One would've thought that after they stole that car, they would have learned their fucking lesson, but I hadn't properly dealt with Wick's ass because they were forcing me with this stupid ass wedding. Now I was 'bout to break his fucking neck. That was the only way he was gon' stop fucking playing with us.

"I'll handle it," I told him and marched toward the door. I exited the building before Streets was able to say anything else. Wick thought he was slick, and that nigga was gon' have to be made an example of. Hopping back into my truck, I instructed my driver to take me to Wick's house. The nigga was so fucking stupid. If he was gon' be out here doing dirt, the least he could do was move his family out that house where we couldn't find 'em.

Fredrick pulled up to Wick's house and I got out the truck before he could open the door. My trigger finger itched, and I was ready to take my frustrations out on his ass. I politely knocked on the door and waited for someone to come to it. Wick's mama opened the door and asked, "Can I help you?"

"I'm looking for your son, Wick. Is he here?"

"He's not in at the moment. You can leave a message if you want, and I'll get it to him soon as he comes in."

"I just might do that. May I come in?" A sinister grin appeared on my face.

"Sure." She stepped to the side and allowed me into her home. "Let me grab a piece of paper and a pen."

She went to walk off, but I told her, "That's not necessary," and closed the gap between us. "Your son has been touching shit that doesn't belong to him. He's been causing me too many problems. He has to know that his choices have consequences." Reaching into my pocket, I pulled out my knife and her eyes expanded as if they were 'bout to pop out of her head.

"Wha-what are you doing?" She slowly backed away from me. With every step she took, I took one as well.

"You said I can leave your son a message and that's exactly what I'm 'bout to do."

"Walter!" she screamed at the top of her lungs and moments later, this guy entered the living room from the back of the house. He was 'bout average height. I could take him if needed to, but I wasn't here to fight a soul. Fighting wasn't in my nature. I pulled triggers and didn't ask questions.

"What the hell is going on in here?" Wick's father asked.

"I'm here to leave a message for your son. You'll do." I turned my frame toward him, and his eyes landed on the knife in my hand.

"I'm gon' tell you one fucking time to get the fuck out of my house."

"Or what?" Stopping in my tracks, I ran my thumb down my blade.

"I'm gon' call the police."

"Call 'em, but I can guarantee you that by the time I get here, you'll be sliced from ear to ear and I'll be long gone."

"What do you want?" Wick's mama asked with tears seeping down her cheeks.

"I told you. I'm just here to leave your son a message. Now which one of you gon' take it?"

Her eyes drifted from me to her husband. Wick's father stepped forward and said, "I will. What's the message."

"Oh, my messages don't work like that. Put your hand down on the table."

"What?"

"You heard me. Put your fucking hand on the table. We can do this the easy way or the hard way."

"Wha-what are you about to do?" Wick's mama questioned me. Had they already done what the fuck I needed 'em to, I could have already been out their fucking hair. Either way, I wasn't leaving here 'til I caused physical harm to his ass.

Wick's father placed his hand down on the table. Lifting mine, I slammed my knife down on his pinky and he screamed out, "Ahhh!" Blood shot from his hand and Wick's mama quickly grabbed a rag and covered his hand.

"Are you fucking insane!" she screamed at me.

"It's just a fucking pinky. He can continue living his life without it. Your son got twenty-four hours to surrender himself or I'll be back to chop off another finger."

"What are you going to do to him?" she questioned me.

"Far worse than chopping a fucking finger. Find your son before you bitches be using your feet for ya hands," I told 'em and treaded out the door.

CHAPTER TWENTY-TWO
COCO
VALENTINE'S DAY

Our vacation was vastly approaching, and I had yet to get all of my outfits together. Honey said something about bringing it back up to Law so she could go. I thought it was bizarre that he was punishing her like she was a child. If that was what marriage like was like, I'on think I ever want that shit.

I had been in class all day long and now I was ready to go home and climb in bed. Since I wasn't seeing anyone, Valentine's was just like another day for me. People had been receiving gifts at school all day long and I felt kinda salty about it. Shit was cute though.

"Ms. Hurts?" Professor Letterman called out my name, bringing me from my thoughts.

"Yeah?" My eyes zeroed in on her at the front of the room as she stood in front of her white board.

"You can daydream at home, not in my class."

I sunk down lower in my seat and waited for all the attention to get off me. There was a knock at the classroom door and this guy entered with a huge bouquet in their hands.

"Can I help you?" Professor Letterman asked him.

"I'm looking for a Coco Hurts." My heart skipped beats in my chest. Professor Letterman glowered at me, and I shot to my feet, collecting my things. She'd already got on me about daydreaming, I wasn't about to catch this lashing too.

"I'm sorry, Professor Letterman," I said as I zoomed past her toward the door. "I'm Coco," I told the guy and pulled him out the door by the forearm.

"I have this for you. Happy Valentine's Day," he said as he handed me the bouquet. I noticed it wasn't a normal one, it was actually made of red roses and books. Books! One of the very things I cherished. Pulling the card from the bouquet, I opened it.

Coco,

I hope this finds you well. I haven't heard anything else from you about our date and it's cool. I'm not rushing anything. I was just letting you know that you're being thought about and even though I never asked you to be my Valentine, you deserve to be happy and feel special on this day. Enjoy the rest of your day.

-Streets

My heart damn near burst in my chest. This man wasn't even my man and he was already going to lengths to make me happy. There was no telling what he'd do if we were actually dating. Pulling out my phone, I texted Honey to see where she was. It's crazy because the only time she was able to have her phone was when she was at school.

Where are you?

As I waited for a response, I scanned the books that Streets bought. They were all urban romance. My favorite genre. My buzzing phone pulled my attention.

Honey: *Cafeteria.*

Shifting my bookbag on my shoulder, I made my way toward the exit to go find Honey. She hadn't told me anything about how she was spending Valentine's Day. Last year, she spent it in her room crying over a fuck nigga that was caught out with another chick that morning. I prayed this one was better for her.

When I entered the cafeteria, I found Honey sitting at one of the tables with Marcia. They were munching on a burger. "Look what just got delivered to my class," I said and turned the bouquet so they could get a good look at it. "Ain't it cute?" My cheeks burned from smiling so hard.

"Who sent you that?" Honey asked and took another bite from her burger then stuffed a fry into her mouth. Sometimes she ate like she hadn't eaten in days. By just staring at her, I swear one wouldn't think she ate like that.

"Streets," I anxiously answered her, and Marcia's head snapped in my direction.

"Are you serious?"

"Yeah. It came to class a few minutes ago."

"Damn, I ain't get shit." Marcia rolled her eyes.

"Last time I checked, you weren't even talking to anyone," Honey said and continued to eat her food.

"What the fuck you got while you're all in my damn business?" Marcia rolled her eyes again.

"I don't know. I haven't been home yet."

"Do y'all have any plans for the night?" I asked her and took my seat at the table.

"He hasn't said anything to me about anything."

"She don't have no plans," Marcia joked.

What's her fucking problem? She was acting real salty over there. Marcia had been weird ever since we got kidnapped that day.

Honey didn't make eye contact with either one of us. "If you don't have any plans, that's cool. The day is about love, not about who can get the most or best gifts."

"Coco, you do realize you're talking to someone who doesn't love her fiancé at all. I barely know the man."

"I guess you got a point there. Well, at least it's almost time for our vacation. I think all of us need it."

Marcia clapped her hands together and said, "I promise I just did a Shein haul. I'm waiting on my clothes now. I'm 'bout to be so fine."

"Did you get a birthday outfit? Are we doing a certain color or theme?" I questioned Honey.

"You can do whatever color you want. I'm just gon' wear whatever I have at the house."

"Why?"

"It's not like I can go out and buy something new and the only time I have my phone is when I leave the house."

"I'on see how you doing it," Marcia added.

"I can look for you some stuff if you want me to," I offered.

"That's not necessary. It's fine."

My phone chimed, alerting me that my next class was about to start. "You sure?" I asked and lifted to my feet.

"Yeah. It's cool."

"Okay, I gotta get to my next class. I'll see y'all later," I said and rushed off.

I scrolled my social media silently on my ride to the house. Everyone was posting all the gifts they got for the day and I prayed that Honey made it home to something. Despite their relationship, she deserved to be celebrated too.

When my driver pulled into the driveway, there was a Rolls Royce parked at the door. He stopped behind it and opened the door for me. I climbed out and the driver of the car got out. "Are you Coco Hurts?"

"Yes."

"I'm your ride for the evening."

"Huh? I didn't order you. I don't have any plans."

"Mr. Streets sent me."

Pulling my phone out, I dialed Streets number to see what the hell was going on. He picked up on the second ring. "Streets, first I want to thank you for the bouquet. Secondly, why is this car in the driveway?"

"It's your ride for the evening. I want to take you on a date for Valentine's Day."

"I thought I told you that I was gon' think about it."

"You did and you still can. If the car pulls up at seven, then I know you want to see where this goes. If not, I'll understand. Enjoy the rest of your night, beautiful," he said and ended the call.

Damn, he was smooth. With the gestures he was making, how could I say no to going out with him? He knew I was celibate, therefore, there was no way he was trying to take me out to fuck. Maybe he genuinely wanted to get to know me. Honestly, I didn't really mind. We vibed when we're together. No way I was about to miss this blessing.

"I'll be right back," I told the driver and went into the house.

"Hey, baby, how was school?" Ma asked soon as I rushed past her for the staircase. "Where you going in a hurry?"

"I have a date."

"Huh? With who?"

Stopping at the top of the stairs, I turned and replied, "Streets Blanco."

"Coco..."

"Ma, not right now. I have to go find me something to wear," were my last words before I jetted for my bedroom.

He wanted me to be somewhere at seven and it was going

on five. I needed to find something to wear, comb my hair, do my makeup, and shower all in this short lil time.

Going into my closet, I searched for the perfect outfit for the night and found this pink rhinestone, strapless bodycon dress that had a split up the right thigh. It was a dress that was purchased for one of Daddy's fundraisers that I didn't get to go to because I ended up catching the flu. Grabbing the dress, I tossed it on the bed and went into the bathroom and started the shower. I was in the bathroom a good forty minutes before I came out and lotioned my body down and sprayed myself with my favorite Versace perfume. It was imperative that I left the house smelling good so that Streets could think about me long after I was in his presence.

After slipping on my panties, I sat down at my vanity and proceeded to do my hair and makeup. The way my dress was made, I wasn't able to wear a bra.

Finishing up my hair, I got up and slipped my dress on and paired it with my silver red-bottom pumps. I stepped to my mirror and was in awe. I'd outdone myself and couldn't wait for Streets to see me. Grabbing my clutch and phone, I exited the bedroom and bumped into Ma in the hallway. She was dressed as well, which I assumed meant she was about to go out with Daddy somewhere. Though he worked so much, he still made it his mission to be there for us every birthday and holiday, even if it wasn't for that much time.

"You look beautiful," she said with a grin.

"So do you. You and Dad have plans?"

"Yeah, he's taking me out to dinner. Be careful with that boy Streets. Don't be out too late."

"Ma, trust me, you don't have anything to worry about," I told her, and we both descended the stairs. Streets knew about my celibacy, and I doubted he'd try anything tonight.

I exited the house and the driver got out the car and

opened the door for me. I slipped into the seat and waited to see exactly where I was going. I'd been on dates before, but it was nothing of this caliber.

After driving for a few minutes, the driver pulled up to Millionaire Suites. "This has to be a mistake," I said as I looked out the window at the building.

"No. This is where I was told to bring you," the driver said as he climbed out the car and opened the back door for me. I stepped out the car and noticed Streets standing on the sidewalk. He stood there dressed in all black. That man was so fucking divine. What really put the icing on the cake was the single pink rose he housed in his hand.

Taking a step in my direction, his lips parted, and he said, "Damn, you look gorgeous."

I diverted my attention to his shiny loafers and fidgeted with a couple stones on my dress. Streets hooked me by the chin and lifted my face. "Don't ever break contact when I'm speaking to you. You're beautiful as hell, Coco. You need to know that." I nodded and he handed me the flower. "For you," he said, and I placed the rose to my nose, taking a whiff.

"Thank you. You're really a gentleman. I don't understand how you're single. The girls are really missing out."

"Maybe I was waiting for you."

"Now you think you smooth." He chuckled.

"Come this way. I want to show you something." He extended his hand in my direction and mine softly fell into it. He escorted me into the building and took me straight to the ballroom.

When he opened the doors, my mouth slacked. This man had the entire ballroom decorated. Straight ahead was a table set for two with candles burning in the center. Red rose petals circled the table in the shape of a heart. To the right of that was a huge projector screen with a white, sheer tent set up in front of it. Inside the tent was a small table was all sorts of snacks on it and two huge bean bag chairs rested behind it.

"I—I don't know what to say."

"You don't have to say anything. We'll start with dinner then we can end the night with a movie. I hope you like what I picked out," he said and led me over to the table. This man even pulled the chair out for me. I wasn't used to any of this treatment at all.

Taking my seat, I waited for what was next. Streets sat across from me. Seconds later, the door opened, and a woman strutted in with two plates in her hands. Streets grabbed the champagne and poured both of us a glass. Luckily that's all it was, or else I would have let him know that I wasn't old enough to drink nor did I like partaking in those activities anyway.

The woman set one of the plates down in front of me. My mouth salivated at the parmesan-covered steak, creamy mashed potatoes, asparagus, and grilled shrimp. I couldn't wait to dig into that food. I'd skipped lunch earlier because I was too fascinated with my bouquet to even think about eating.

Hopefully he doesn't think I'm a pig.

I sat there and observed Streets as he lowered his head to say grace over his food. It was insane that he did that and was able to take another person's life.

Once he was done, he grabbed his knife and sliced his steak. "Did I pick a good choice in food?"

Picking up my fork and knife, I responded, "Yes. It looks delicious. I want to thank you again for the bouquet. You really put a lot of thought into it. The books were an excellent choice."

Streets beamed a smile at me. "I remembered how you told me that you loved to read. If I was gon' do something, it might as well have been something thoughtful."

"You get points for that." I placed a piece of steak in my mouth and moaned. "Mmhmm." It tasted better than I could ever imagine.

We sat there and had small talk over dinner then moved over to the movie. It surprised the hell out of me when I saw the movie he chose for us to watch. He picked out this movie call *Paper Heart*. I'd read the book a while ago and loved it but never got around to watching the movie.

Once the movie was over, Streets took me straight home. He walked me up to the front door and we stood there on the porch, gazing at each other. Truthfully, I didn't want the night to end.

"I had a really good time," I told him.

"Me too. I'm glad you did. That means I can get another date, right?"

Snickering, I replied, "We'll see." I went to open the door, but he caught me by the wrist, stopping me.

"Can I kiss you?"

I nipped my lower lip as I stared at his lips. It had been something I'd been thinking about for a while now but didn't know how to go about it. I nodded and his hand snaked around my waist, meshing our bodies. My heartbeat throbbed in my throat. His lips neared mine but before we could kiss, headlights shone on us, and we peeled apart. My parents climbed out the truck and neared us.

"Streets," Ma called out his name.

"Good evening, Ms. Hurts, Governor Hurts." Daddy mugged him but didn't speak a word as he brushed past us into the house.

"I'm going to get going. Thanks again," I said as I rushed into the house and shut the door behind me. Streets saw the pure authentic me. He didn't care that I was celibate. Everything he did was to truly get to know me.

CHAPTER TWENTY-THREE
HONEY

When I came home, the house was empty. I'd snuck off from my security detail to enjoy a lil freedom before I had to come back to this prison. Law blew my phone up while I was gone, and I'd ignored every call. Whatever the consequences were when I got here, I was just gon' have to deal with.

There wasn't a single flower or piece of candy waiting for me. What did I expect? I was with a man who told me upfront not to look for any affection because he wasn't giving it. That was the main reason why I wasn't in a rush to make it home. It was lonely and depressing. Our birthday trip couldn't come fast enough. I had yet to let it be known that Law had already told me I wouldn't be attending because I had every intention of asking him again. No wasn't an option.

"Are you hungry?" Nigel questioned me when I entered the kitchen. My stomach was touching my back actually.

"What's for dinner?"

"Tilapia and grits."

"Yeah, I can eat." I made my way toward the dining room

and took a seat at the huge table. Nigel brought my plate out to me, and I sat there, glowering at the empty seat at the head of the table. "Happy Valentine's Day," I said, mumbling underneath my breath. This couldn't be how I was spending the rest of my life. Something was gon' have to give.

Picking up my fork, I began to eat my food. The fork clacking against the plate was driving me insane. Grabbing the plate, I lunged it at his chair, and it shattered.

"I fucking hate you!"

Nigel appeared in the doorway and asked, "Is everything okay?"

Warm tears soaked my cheeks. "It's fine. I'm going to bed," I said and stepped away from the table. Nigel began to clean up the mess I made and I halted. "You don't ever get lonely here?" I turned and questioned him.

Pausing with a piece of glass in his hand, he looked over his shoulder and replied, "It beats being alone. I've been working for the Blancos for the last thirty years. I don't have no other family. This is my family."

My face scrunched. "How can someone so cruel be your family?"

"Law isn't as bad as you think."

"Nigel, it's Valentine's Day and he's purposely forcing me to spend it alone just like any other day."

Sighing, he straightened his posture and faced me. "You have to break that ice around his heart. Deep down, Law is just someone who wants to be loved but is scared of it. Don't let him fool you. He's not pushing you away to hurt you, he's keeping you at a distance to keep from hurting himself."

"I guess that makes sense. I'm going to my room. Sorry for the mess."

"It's my job. Have a good night, Ms. Honey."

As I climbed the stairs to my bedroom, my phone began to

ring. Thinking it was Law again, I pulled it from my pocket and went to press the ignore button 'til I saw it was Coco.

"You okay?" I immediately answered.

"Girl, Streets took me on a date and oh my God, it was everything." Shutting my bedroom door behind me, I kicked my shoes off and pulled my shirt over my head. "That man is so full of surprises. I'm starting to like him."

"I'm glad you had a good day. You deserve it."

"How was yours though?"

Not wanting to dampen her mood, I lied, "It was cool. I'm just getting in."

"I'm so glad this one was better than last year. You deserve so much, Honey. You're always putting everybody before you. I just really want you to be happy. I know it's hard being with someone like Law, but I pray that one day you two grow to love each other. I'd never be able to live with myself knowing you were miserable for the rest of your life."

Moisture filled the brims of my eyes, but I refused to let the tears fall. "Thanks, Coco. I'm going to get ready for bed. I'll see you tomorrow."

"Kay."

The call disconnected, and I tossed my phone onto the bed. Maybe I wasn't able to get my happily ever after, but Coco just might get hers, and I was cool with that.

CHAPTER TWENTY-FOUR
STREETS
A COUPLE DAYS LATER

Ever since Coco's and my date, it'd been the only thing I could think about. She looked beautiful as hell, and I hated the night had to end, but I didn't want to keep her out too late. I couldn't wait 'til we were able to spend more time together. The ball was in her court. When she wanted to see me, she'd let me know. For now, it was back to business.

I pulled into the parking lot of Blanco's and parked at the front door. It was the middle of the day and I wanted to see how things were running with the new security detail. The guys I hired were the best of the best. The next mufucka that decided they wanted to rob us was in for a rude awakening.

Getting out the car, I went into the building. Two men stood in there with assault rifles strapped to their backs, one at the entrance and the other by the counter.

Hitting 'em with a head nod, I sauntered over to the door and unlocked it. "Y'all good?" I asked the girls. When I hired the new security, I didn't know how they were gon' feel 'bout the weapons, but I was doing whatever necessary to ensure their safety.

"Yeah, we okay," Tiffany answered.

"I was just stopping by to check on y'all. I'm finna head out, but if you need anything, don't be afraid to hit my line." They both nodded and I exited the room, making sure to lock the door behind me.

As I stepped out the building, I hit Law up to see what he was up to. He'd been particularly quiet lately, more than usual, and that's not like him.

"Wassup?" he answered, and I slipped into the seat of my truck.

"What the hell you been up to? I was just leaving the main store checking up on shit."

"Been searching for Wick's ass. Nigga ain't showed up after I left his parents a message. I'm 'bout to head over there now."

"You want me to meet you there?"

"If you want. I gotta leave his ass another message to let him know I ain't fucking 'round. The nigga hiding out somewhere 'cause he knows we're looking for him. I gotta find that nigga before he tries to slip out of town."

"I'll be there," I told him and ended the call. "Take me to Wick's house," I told my driver and got comfortable for the ride.

By the time I made it there, Law's truck was pulling into the driveway. There were no other cars there. We climbed out and headed up to the front door. Law lifted his foot and kicked the door off the hinges.

"What you did that for?"

"The mufuckas ain't here. There was no need to knock. The mufucka probably got them out of here 'cause he knows we're on his ass. I should have just held 'em hostage 'til his stupid ass showed his face. This my fuck up," he said as he stepped into the house. Shit was thrown everywhere, which only meant they left in a hurry. Pieces of clothes left a trail from the hallway to the couch. Law was right, they were long gone and there's no telling where they were by now. "The only way I'll be able to get my hands on Wick's bitch ass is through Dash."

Law marched out the house and jumped into his truck before I was able to say anything else. He was going after Dash as if he had something to do with that bullshit, and that's the exact reason why I was heading to the governor's house to stop him from killing him.

Law's driver dashed through the streets with my truck directly behind him. We made it to the governor's house in no time. When we got there, he ran up the steps and entered the house as if he was welcome. By the time Law was done here today, he was probably never gon' be allowed to step foot in this house again.

"Dash!" Law barked. He was angry as hell. That's the only time he ever raised his voice.

"What's going on?" Coco appeared at the top of the stairs in a skintight gray jumpsuit. I had to remove my eyes from her pussy print. Her hair was slicked back in a ponytail at the nape of her neck.

"Is your brother here?" I asked her, and she nodded.

"I'll go get him."

Coco zoomed from the top of the stairs and moments later came back with Dash who wiped sleep from his eyes.

"Where the fuck is Wick?" Law wasted no time questioning him as he approached the staircase. Being the smart person he was, Dash came down to the last stair to avoid rolling involuntarily.

"I don't know. I haven't talked to him in a few days."

Law roughly gripped Dash by the collar of his t-shirt and said, "Tell me all the places I can find that mufucka besides home. He's hiding and I gotta find him."

"Damn, you gotta be so aggressive? I would have told you

what you needed to know without roughing me up." Dash frowned and Law loosened his grip on him.

"Talk."

"The only places I know he'd be is at this chick house he's been fucking. Her name is Chasity. She stays out there in Tulane Court. If he's not there, then you can try a few places where he hangs out frequently. The Game Room, G's, and the Boom Boom Room."

"That nigga ain't old enough to get into any of those places."

Dash's eyes darted in my direction. "That don't stop him from being in there."

"If you hear anything from that nigga, let me know," were Law's last words before he marched out of the house.

"Can I go back to sleep now?" Dash asked me, and I nodded.

He went back upstairs, passing Coco along the way. She watched him for a second then came down to meet me at the bottom of the stairs.

"Your brother is a hot head."

"I know." The tips of my fingers stroked some loose strands of hair back out her face. Her eyes bored into mine, and my heart palpitated. Coco was the only woman walking this earth that was capable of making my heart skip beats. "I've been thinking 'bout you."

"Have you really?" She grinned so hard, displaying her perfect teeth.

"Yeah. I hate we didn't get to finish what we started the other night." Gripping her hand, I pulled her into my frame, and she melted. My eyes drifted to her lips. "I need to know how those feel." It was driving me insane.

Palming my face, she closed her eyes and meshed our lips. Coco's lips felt as if I was falling into a fluffy cloud. Her mouth slightly parted, and I nested my tongue against hers. We kissed long and hard 'til we both were out of breath. My forehead rested against hers, eyes still closed, not wanting the moment to come to an end.

My vibrating phone separated us. Pulling it out, I saw that it was a text from Mama Ada. "I gotta go," I told Coco and pecked her once more on the lips before exiting the house.

CHAPTER TWENTY-FIVE
HONEY
A WEEK LATER

I sat there on the foot of the bed, debating if I wanted to leave the house or not. Law was angry as fuck with me about the shit I pulled on Valentine's Day, but who could blame me? He came in the next morning and took my phone away and said I wasn't getting it back 'til he felt like giving it back. I could see that every time I did something he didn't like, he was gon' try to find a way to punish me as if I was a fucking child.

Today, I was being forced to spend time with Law for the first time in a while. Mama Ada had booked us dance classes to take. I thought it was stupid as fuck. I knew how to dance for the most part, but I didn't know how to do any of that fancy ass shit I assumed they were gon' be looking for me to do at the wedding. For the longest, I had been trying to figure out a way to get out of it but came up empty-handed.

A knock at my bedroom door broke my thoughts. Nigel poked his head in the room with his eyes closed. "Are you decent?" he asked, and I snickered.

"Yes."

His eyes shot open, and he said, "Your ride is here. Do you need anything before you go?"

"No, I'm fine. Thanks." Getting up from the bed, I grabbed my Louis Vuitton bag and trotted in his direction. The sooner I got to this bullshit, the quicker I could get back home to my sanity. Being around Law, I was certain he was gon' trigger me and all hell was gon' break loose. It bothered me that the only thing he was worried about on Valentine's Day was the fact that I hadn't been answering the phone and didn't come straight home like I was supposed to. He didn't even bother to offer me a late happy Valentine's Day or anything.

When I got outside, the driver opened the back door for me and I climbed into the car. I was getting really sick and tired of these people having to drive me everywhere I needed to go. For once, I just wished I could walk out the door and climb into my own car. The life I was about to live, I was certain that was a luxury I'd never get to experience. Ever since I came into this world, I had yet to see any of them drive themselves. It was sad actually.

The driver pulled up to Nice Dance Studios and I got out the truck. Law's ride was already there as well as what I assumed was Mama Ada's. No way she was about to let me embarrass myself in peace.

When I entered the building, I saw that the only people in there were Law, Mama Ada, Coco, Streets, and the woman who was supposed to teach us how to dance. When I was told that I had to come to this, I didn't know they were forcing Coco and nem as well. I didn't even see the point in learning how to dance for one day. It shouldn't really matter if we stepped on each other's toes for a few seconds.

"Now that everyone is finally here, we can get started," the woman said and grabbed her phone off the rectangular table. I figured she was searching for soothing music when I heard a song began to play lowly in the background. "Grab your partners."

I eyed Law as he sat in one of the chairs with his phone shoved up to his face. Coco and Streets lifted to their feet and lustfully gazed at each other. Seeing my sister this happy warmed my heart. Law rose to his feet and shoved his phone down into his pocket. With every step he took in my direction, my heart banged in my chest. This was gon' be the closest we'd been since we took those pictures at the engagement party.

Law stopped in front of me, and I rubbed up and down my arm as I waited for our next instructions. "We're starting off with something simple." Stepping behind me, she pushed me into Law's arms and my breath caught in my throat. She positioned my left hand on his shoulder and my right in his left. Law's dark eyes pored into mine as we waited for instructions. The way the family carried themselves, one would've thought they already knew how to dance.

"We're taking small steps on count. One, two, three. One, two, three."

Our bodies began to move to her voice and before I knew it, I caught the hang of it. It wasn't really that bad. She took her attention over to Coco and Streets where Coco seemed to not be able to stop stepping on his toes. I giggled every time I saw him jump back out my peripheral.

Law was quiet, not making a peep, so I decided to break the ice. "Is this really how things are going to be between us for the rest of our lives?" All he hit me with was a shrug. "I don't appreciate how you left me all alone for Valentine's Day. You forced me to sit there and have dinner by myself. The least you could've did was shown up."

"You're right." I stepped on his shoe, surprised by his response, and he yanked his foot back. "I have been treating you poorly, and I apologize for that."

"I'm hearing things, right?"

"I can take that shit right back."

"Okay. Okay."

We finished up our dance lesson and Law wasted no time getting the hell out of there. I lingered around for a bit with Coco, knowing that once I made it back to the house, I was stuck.

"I really like Streets for you. He seems like he makes you happy," I told her as we sat there and watched Streets dance with Mama Ada.

"He really does."

"So are y'all dating now?"

"I'm not sure. We went on one date and that was it."

"Don't you think you need to be finding out what y'all have going on?"

"I will," she answered and focused her attention on Streets.

"I'm going to head on to the house," I told her and got up from my seat. I embraced her, grabbed my purse, and left out of there. It was a few things I wanted to look into before Law came back around.

After I found that bedroom in his closet, I had been trying to do my research on that sort of thing. I had gone down the BDSM rabbit hole. Let's just say, I came across a lot of shit. I was no sex expert, so I decided to bribe the driver into taking me by the sex store so I could talk to one of them.

"Can you take me by Love Stuff?" I asked him soon as I came out the door and he opened the back door for me.

"You know that we're only allowed to take you to approved places. You'll have to call and get permission from Mr. Blanco."

"Either you fucking take me there or I'll call and tell him how you be sleep on the fucking job. How else I lost you Valentine's Day?"

Groaning, he said, "Fine. Five minutes then I'm getting you back to the house."

"That's all I need."

He shut the door on me and climbed into the driver's seat. On the way to the sex store, I tried to piece together all the questions I wanted to ask once I got in there. By the time those five minutes were over, I wanted to be fluent in BDSM. If I was marrying this man and being stuck with him for the rest of my life, I had to know what I was getting myself into.

We arrived at the store and I went inside. "ID," was the first thing to escape the woman's lips behind the counter.

I slipped my ID across the counter to her and she handed it right back. "Let me know if you need help with anything."

"Actually, I do. What can you tell me about BDSM? I just recently found out that my fiancé is into that sort of thing. I've been looking up some of it online, but I don't have a clear understanding."

"BDSM has different practices. Do you know which form he's into?"

"Not really. I found a bedroom with all types of stuff in it. I haven't really talked to him about it, but if I'm going to marry him, I need to know what I'm getting myself into. Is it crazy that once I looked up the porn, it turned me on?"

"Do you think that you're into it as well?"

"I don't know what I like. I'm still a virgin."

"Ahh, I see. Dabbling in BDSM fresh out of your virginity can be a lil hardcore. You need to find out exactly what your man is into. They also be having some parties in Atlanta if you ever want to go to one."

"Eww, no."

Covering her mouth, she snickered. "You don't have to participate. It's just something to give you an idea of what you're getting yourself into. We have a few movies over there as well if you want to check one out."

"Thanks, but I think I'll just stick to online," I told her and left out the store before that annoying ass driver came in there searching for me.

On my way home, I went onto porn sites and searched BDSM. The way the women were in bondage and getting spanked made my pussy twitch. Maybe God knew what he was doing when he placed us together. Had I not stumbled upon that room, I probably would have never known that sort of stuff turned me on.

CHAPTER TWENTY-SIX
LAW
A COUPLE DAYS LATER

For whatever reason, Honey has been on my mind heavily after our lil dance lesson. She was right, I had been treating her unfairly as if it was her fault we were in this shit. Had I gone out and found my own bride like Pops told me long ago, she wouldn't have ever gotten dragged into this shit.

Gripping Lala's mane, I guided her up and down on my dick. My eyes closed and my head rested back against the cushion. Honey's beautiful face appeared in my mind. From the way she wrinkled her nose whenever she was angry to that sexy ass smile of hers. It was killing me slowly. Lala's brain was supposed to pull me away from the bullshit, but it was as if it was drawing me to her further. Fuck.

"This shit ain't working," I said and yanked her mouth off my dick by the hair.

"What's wrong?" she asked and wiped her mouth with the back of her hand.

"Got too much shit on my mind. I'on wanna talk 'bout it."

Shoving my dick back down into my pants, I got up from the couch.

"That's cool. Maybe next time I can toss this pussy at you." The corner of her mouth quirked. I had yet to tell Lala that I was about to get married. She probably already knew this because the shit was all over social media and damn near the only thing people seemed to talk about in Montgomery and the surrounding areas. The beautiful governor's daughter and mysterious billionaire bachelor were to be wed in the spring. Everyone and their mama were trying their best to get on the invitation list just to be nosey and see how everything turned out.

"I'on know if there will be a next time. I'm 'bout to get married," I casually told her.

"And you just now tell me this?"

At first, I had no plans on ever saying anything because I still planned on fucking her long after Honey and I tied the knot, but Honey's ass had been getting underneath my skin. She changed my total thought process, and I wasn't certain if that was bad or good.

"What's the issue? We were just having fun."

"It still would've been nice to know that you're getting married." Folding her arms over her chest, she frowned. Shawty was already getting fucking attached and we hadn't even been messing 'round long. Guess it was a good thing I did speak up.

"I'm 'bout to head out," I told her. The conversation was heading in a direction that I didn't feel like dealing with.

"So this the last time I'm gon' see you?" Lala stomped behind me as I went out the door. "You don't hear me fucking talking to you!"

"Watch ya fucking tone when speaking to me," I told her over my shoulder as I neared my truck.

"This stupid as fuck! I shouldn't have ever started fucking with you!"

Ignoring her, I climbed into the truck and my driver shut the door in her face. We were backed out her driveway in no time and headed straight to the house. It was rolling around five thirty by the time I made it there. Honey was more than likely in the dining room having dinner. Since I hadn't eaten anything yet, I made my way in there to eat with her. One would've thought it was Christmas time the way Honey's eyes lit up when she spotted me. Nigel excused himself from the room to go grab me a plate as I got comfortable at the head of the table.

"I'm surprised to see you here," she softly spoke.

"Can I not have dinner with my fiancée?"

"Since when?"

"Since now..." Nigel rested a plate down in front of me. "Thank you." Nodding, he stepped back into his place, waiting for me and Honey to finish our dinner.

As I stuffed a forkful of pasta into my mouth, my eyes wandered down to Honey. Her face glowed as if the moon shone down through the ceiling on her.

"I'm actually glad that you're here." Her gaze synced with mine.

"How come?"

"I wanted to talk to you about something." Resting my fork against the plate, I gave her my undivided attention. "As you know, Coco and my birthday trip is coming up and I was wondering if you'd—"

"No," I interrupted her.

"But you didn't let me finish my question."

"Go 'head," I told her and picked my fork back up, already knowing that my answer wasn't gon' change.

"I was wondering if you'd let me go. It's our twenty-first birthday. We have to do something to celebrate it."

"You should've thought 'bout that shit when you tried to kill me."

"How can you blame me though? Look how you were treating me, then the contract states that it'll be void if something was to happen to you. I just wanted my freedom."

"And what about now?"

Honey placed her fork in her mouth and chewed as if she needed time to think about the question I'd asked her. "I don't know," she finally answered. "So you're really not gon' let me go on my trip?"

"The answer is no," I told her for the final time.

Sucking her teeth, she got up from the table and left out of the dining room. At least she wasn't fighting being here anymore. Maybe we were finally getting somewhere.

CHAPTER TWENTY-SEVEN
COCO
A COUPLE DAYS LATER

"You sure you have everything you need?" Ma asked me from the doorway as I zipped my suitcase. I wasn't certain why I'd waited 'til the day of to pack my things, knowing I'd probably leave something, but whatever I was missing, I'd get when we got to Bali.

"I think so."

Moisture filled her eyes as she stared at me. "I really can't believe that my baby girls are about to be twenty-one. Time really does fly."

"It really does," I agreed with her. In just a few hours, Honey and I were finally gon' be legal.

"Just make sure that y'all call and check in once you make it there."

"We will," I promised her and pecked her on the cheek then grabbed my suitcase from the bed. "Where's Daddy?"

"He had some meeting this morning but told me to tell you that he loves you."

"I'm sure he did," I mumbled and left out the room.

Soon as I made it downstairs, my driver grabbed my

luggage from me and carried it out to the truck. "I'm picking up Honey," I told him and climbed into the back seat. Pulling out my phone, I shot her a text to let her know that I was on my way. After Valentine's Day, Law finally gave her phone privileges back, and she was happy as hell too because she wasn't dying from boredom any longer.

When we pulled up to her house, I called her phone. "I'm outside."

"Okay, give me a few minutes. I'll be right out," she said and disconnected the call.

I scrolled for a bit on my social media as I waited for Honey and saw that Marcia had posted about her getting ready to catch a flight. This was about to be one long ass trip. First we had to drive all the way to Atlanta just to catch a one-way flight. After that, we were gon' be on a plane for a day and some hours. We were literally gon' bring our birthday in on a plane.

When I looked up from my phone, I saw Honey running out the house with her suitcase rolling behind her. The driver got out, and she tossed her luggage at him. I pushed the back door open for her, and she jumped into the truck.

"I take it that Law doesn't know you're leaving."

"Nope. I asked him again and he said no." She shrugged and Nigel stopped at the front door, calling out her name.

"Ms. Honey!"

"Just act like you don't see him and pull off."

The driver pulled out the driveway and headed for Marcia's house.

"Has Marcia been acting strange to you lately?" Honey questioned me when we were halfway to her house.

"A lil bit. What do you think that's all about?"

"I don't know, but I'm damn sure gon' find out."

The driver pulled into Marcia's driveway and she was

already outside with her bags. She tossed them into the trunk and got in across from us.

"I can't wait to get out there on the water. You did book us a yacht, right?"

"Yes, Marcia."

"Good. I'm finna make everybody jealous with my posts the entire trip."

"Y'all can just unplug me once we make it to Atlanta," I told them and opened my Kindle. I downloaded several audiobooks for this trip, and I was about to escape into their worlds.

BALI

"What's wrong?" I asked Honey as we waited for our bags. She pressed the power button on her phone and slipped it into her pocket.

"Law's calling nonstop."

"Yeah, 'cause he realizes that you're not home and is trying to figure out where you are. Why don't you just answer and tell the man what he already knows. Maybe he'll stop calling."

"Or maybe he'd force me onto the next flight home," she said, bending to grab her suitcase.

"And how exactly will he do that over the phone?" My brow arched to my hairline.

"'Cause she does everything he says like a lil puppet." Marcia rolled her eyes.

"Okay, are you gon' tell me where all this hostility is coming from lately? It's really getting on my nerves," Honey spoke up.

"I'm just saying, Honey, I miss the old you before you got engaged to that party pooper. All y'all do is kill all the fun now.

I'm sick of it," she replied and grabbed her bags. "Can we get the hell out of here?"

"Whatever."

We headed toward the exit where I saw a guy dressed in a black suit standing with a sign that read *Hurts Twins*. "That's us," I said, pointing in his direction.

"Are you the Hurts twins?" the guy asked. He was tanned with jet-black hair, fine pink lips, and a goatee. Dude was fine as hell.

"Yes," Honey answered.

"Oh you fine, fine," Marcia said, taking the words right out of my mouth. "You single?" she asked him and locked arms with him as we exited the airport. Waiting outside for us was a black Escalade. The guy and Marcia placed our bags into the trunk while we got comfortable in the truck. "What's our first order of business?" Marcia asked soon as she got inside.

"I think we all should catch up on sleep. I'm jetlagged," Honey spoke and checked her phone for the millionth time.

"Are you serious? I didn't come all the way out here just to sleep," Marcia shot back.

"It's just one day. We're here for a whole week. I got sleep on the plane, but I need some sleep too," I added.

"Whatever." Marcia rolled her eyes and placed her AirPods in her ears.

I enjoyed the view as we headed to our hotel. Honey didn't tell me exactly where we were staying. Since everything was up to her to book, I didn't ask any questions.

The truck went down this dirt road and all I saw were trees and bushes. My head snapped in Honey's direction. Her face was too far inside her phone to even tell that I was looking at her. Her forehead wrinkled, and I knew she had to be stressing about Law. If she was gon' be this on edge, we could've just stayed in the states.

The truck stopped at this beautiful ass villa. Whole time, I thought we were staying in a regular hotel. Of course, Honey was gon' go all out with the trip. According to her, we only turned twenty-one once in our life and she had Law's black card to pay for everything.

We got out the car and two guys approached us. They grabbed our bags out the trunk and carried them inside the villa. It was so beautiful out here. We sat directly on the clear blue water. I couldn't wait to get out there and soak up some sun.

We entered the villa and each chose our bedrooms. As I unpacked my suitcase, Marcia stopped at my door dressed in her bathing suit with a towel draped over her shoulder. "I'm heading to the beach for a bit since you two grandmammies wanna sleep y'all life away."

"Don't forget to put on some sunscreen or yo' ass gon' be burnt to a crisp."

"Damn." Marcia rushed away from my door, and I snickered. She was too ready to get her ass outside that she hadn't even put on any sunscreen. Shit, I wasn't leaving the villa without any on. It didn't matter where we were going. I burned easily and I wasn't going back home not being able to touch my skin without wincing.

Once I was done unpacking, I went to check on Honey. That girl was knocked the fuck out in the bed with her suitcase resting alongside her. She was so tired that she didn't bother to do anything else. Stepping away from her room, I took a short tour of the villa and found myself standing on the back patio that stretched out over the ocean. Honey really did her big one with this one. The wind lightly beat against my skin, and I shut my eyes, taking a huge whiff of the water. Yeah, this vacation was gon' be one to remember.

CHAPTER TWENTY-EIGHT
STREETS
BACK IN THE UNITED STATES

Coco told me how she was going on a birthday trip with her best friend and Honey. She didn't exactly tell me where she was going, but I couldn't wait 'til she made it back so we could spend a lil more time with each other.

As I sat there on my bed, I went to her social media to see what she was up to and if there were any more hints about shit she liked. If I was gon' go after Coco, I had to come correct. She wasn't a regular girl.

My phone chimed and I saw it was a message from Law.

Law: *I need to get in contact with Coco. I can't find Honey.*

Me: *You didn't know they went on vacation?*

My phone instantly began to ring after that message. "Yeah?"

"I told her ass that she wasn't going anywhere. The fuck you mean she on vacation?"

"Coco just told me that she was going on vacation for her birthday. If you can't reach her, then she's probably with her."

"Did she say where she was going?"

"She didn't say."

"Where you at?"

"The house."

"I'm on my way over there," he said and disconnected the call.

Once he said that, I just knew it was 'bout to be some shit. Honey went against Law, that nigga was angry as hell.

Getting up from the bed, I went into the bathroom to handle my hygiene before he showed up at the house. If he was on his way over here, ain't no telling what that nigga was 'bout to do and I needed to be prepared.

By the time I got out the shower and got dressed, Law was calling my phone to let me know he was outside. I opened the door for him, and he marched straight into the house. "Call Coco," he instructed me.

"I'm not sure if she's gon' answer the phone. It's late over there right now. They probably out celebrating."

"I don't give a damn. Call her fucking phone and see where the fuck she's at."

"Alright."

Grabbing my phone off the nightstand, I dialed Coco's number to see if she'd answer the phone. It rang and went to voicemail. "She's not answering."

Law's jaw muscles clenched. "Honey probably told her not to answer the phone for you. I'm gon' kill her."

"Did she use your card to pay for the trip? If she did, you can just call and see where she swiped it at."

"I'on know why I didn't think 'bout that."

Law whipped his phone out and immediately went to call his credit card company. I plopped on the edge of the bed and waited for him to get off the phone to see what he had to say. He stepped out my bedroom for privacy. Maybe he was being a lil harsh on her 'bout stopping her from going out to celebrate for her birthday. It had been something she'd been planning for a while, but who was I to say anything to him. That was his relationship to deal with.

Law came back into the room with a mug resting on his face. "What happened?" I wasted no time to ask him.

"She's in fucking Bali."

"Man, you might as well gone and let her have her lil fun then deal with her ass when she gets back."

"I'll be the judge of that," he said and left out the bedroom.

CHAPTER TWENTY-NINE
HONEY
THE NEXT NIGHT IN BALI

We spent most of the day at the beach. Law was steady calling my phone and I just turned it off completely and placed it in the drawer. He wasn't about to ruin my trip for me. Whatever the consequences were, I'd deal with them once I made it back. This man was trying his best to reach me so bad that he had Streets calling Coco's phone. I told her if she answered that phone, I'd shove that shit down her throat and she could talk to him through her belly button.

The calls had simmered down, and we were preparing to go out for the night. Bali's night life was supposed to be amazing, and I couldn't wait to get to this club that I booked up a section at. Coco wasn't really in the mood to do the entire club scene, but because it was our birthday, she decided to come out with us.

I had damn near tossed all my clothes over my room in search of something cute to put on for the night. Curse Law's ass for telling me that I couldn't come in the first place. I could've easily ordered a haul of clothes and wouldn't be going through this shit.

"Finally," I said, mumbling as I held this long-sleeved, zebra-striped mesh jumpsuit. Thanks to the flex rods I'd been sporting all day, my hair was gon' be looking like I'd just got it done.

After getting dressed, I went into Coco's room to check on her. This girl was sitting at the foot of her bed in her bra and panties. Her silk scarf was still on her head. It was as if she had no plans on getting dressed to go out with us.

"Where are your clothes?"

"Over there." She nodded toward the black dress that rested on the back of the chair in her room.

"Do you plan on putting it on?" My brows snapped together. If it was gon' be like pulling teeth to get her to go out with us, she could stay here.

"I was about to get dressed."

"You sure? If you really don't want to go, you can just stay here."

"No. I came here to partake in birthday activities and that's exactly what I'm gon' do. I was just checking something on my phone right quick."

"Please tell me it wasn't Streets' text messages."

"No," she lied. From the redness of her cheeks, I could sense she wasn't telling the truth.

"Get dressed so we can go. I'm 'bout to take a shot."

"Can you stop fucking playing and just answer the phone," Marcia said as I passed her room. She'd been really secretive with the person she'd been talking to lately and that just wasn't like her. Honestly, almost everything about Marcia lately had been off. Not wanting to pry into her conversation, I went on into the kitchen to grab the bottle of Casamigos we bought earlier that day and took a shot. Soon, Marcia and Coco appeared, and we were ready to go.

The driver took us out to the club. Since I already had us a section booked, we didn't have to wait in line. The bouncer allowed us access straight into the club. The music was lit. I wasn't certain who the artist was that was playing, but I bobbed my head to the music as we maneuvered through the crowd to find our section.

Marcia wasted no time calling the bottle girl over to order us some liquor. Coco got comfortable on the couch where she most likely was gon' spend the entire night. The bottle girl came back with our bottles and sparklers shooting from them. She placed them down on the table and exited our section. As I went to grab a bottle, I felt someone tap my shoulder from behind. When I turned around, I saw this tall, chocolate brother standing there with a huge smirk on his face.

"I noticed the sparklers. What are you celebrating?" My eyes zoomed over his fit. He was draped in Balenciaga from head to toe with two large chains dangling around his neck. He seemed like he'd have a good time and that was the only reason why I didn't turn his ass away. I damn sure wasn't worried about his money because I had my own, whether it was my credit card or the one Law had given me.

"It's our birthday." I nodded in Coco's direction. She sat there with her phone shoved up to her face. Sometimes I hated whenever she got to really liking someone because it was as if she deposited all her time into them.

"Happy birthday," he said over the loud music.

"Thanks."

"How 'bout the next round be on me?"

Shrugging, I lifted the Patrón bottle to my lips and chugged from it. "I'm Honey by the way. That's my sister Coco and Marcia."

Marcia was too busy in this other guy's face to notice the one who was in mine. Knowing her, she was trying to secure her some dick for the evening. We were in a foreign country, and I wasn't with bringing strangers back to where we were laying our head. If she wanted to fuck him, she was gon' have to do it here or outside, but he wasn't coming back with us.

The guy ordered us another round and we partied in the section for a while. Marcia was fucking hammered, and I was a lil tipsy, so Coco thought it was best we went back to the villa. Holding onto Marcia, I staggered a bit as we headed for the exit.

"Do you want me to come along to make sure y'all make it home safe?" the guy asked as we stepped out onto the pavement.

"No thank you," Coco quickly answered for us. "She's engaged anyway, so don't think about it."

"How come this my first time hearing 'bout it?"

Stopping in my tracks, I faced him and asked, "Don't tell me that you think because you bought a few drinks that you thought you were gon' get some?" Snickering, I patted the side of his face.

The driver got out and opened the door for us. Coco helped me get Marcia in the truck while the guy stood back on the sidewalk mugging us. I figured he was gon' get the wrong impression when I allowed him to hang around us for as long as he did. No one was getting this pussy but my husband, and even then, I wasn't certain if he was.

We made it back to the villa and I helped Marcia into bed before heading to my room. I made a U-turn and went into the kitchen to find something to snack on since my stomach began to rumble. The only thing I could find in there was fruit. I made a quick fruit bowl and bounced to my bedroom. Shutting the door behind me, I flipped the switch and the bowl dropped to the floor along with my heart.

"Law?... Wha-what are you doing here? And how come you're sitting in the dark like a crazy person?" Law sat there in the chair in the corner of my room with his elbows resting on his thighs and hands clasped together. He sported this black Versace shorts set. The top wasn't buttoned. This man looked like a fucking sculpture. I promise it was the sexiest shit I'd ever seen.

"You disobeyed a direct order." I swallowed hard the lump that formed in my throat. Though I knew there were gon' be consequences when I returned for leaving when he told me not to, I didn't know what that punishment was gon' be. My hands began to clam. My mouth dryer than cotton as I stared down this man in the face. "Do you know what happens when you disobey me?"

Licking my chap lips, I shook my head. Law straightened his posture and tightly gripped the black paddle that sat on the table next to him. My mind was so focused on him that I hadn't even seen it 'til now.

"C'mere," escaped his lips, and my entire body went rigid.

"Wha-what are you about to do?"

"I won't say it again."

Without further hesitation, I closed the gap between us. My eyes fell under Law's trance as he patted his lap and said, "Lay down, ass up."

"Huh?"

"Did I stutter?"

Not wanting to piss him off any further, I placed my frame over his lap. The paddle clacked against the table as he lifted it. My body tensed from the first smack to my ass. It stung a bit, but I got more pleasure out of it than pain.

Wham!

That time I felt the wind from the paddle before it impacted my ass.

Wham!

"Mmhmm," a moan escaped my lips.

What the fuck is happening to me?

My heartbeat thumped through my pussy.

"You can get up now." I straightened my posture and lustfully gazed at this man. How the hell did I just get whupped for going against his wishes and like it? "From now on, every time you defy me, you'll get spanked."

Cupping Law's face, I swiftly straddled him and crushed my lips against his. Gripping me by the shoulders, he pushed me back. "What are you doing?"

"I—" was the only thing that could form from my lips. Without uttering another word, I rushed into the bathroom and locked the door behind me. Turning on the shower, I paced the floor, brushing my hair back out my face. "What the fuck?" I said, mumbling where Law couldn't hear me.

Stopping in my tracks, I pushed my jumpsuit and thongs down to find them drenched. My pussy was calling Law's name and I didn't know what the fuck to do. Nothing like that had ever happened to me before. Sure, some men have turned me on where I wanted to try to see what sex was like, but Law had me ready to risk it all.

I glided my hand down my abdomen over my pelvis and bald pussy to my clit. My eyes closed and all I could picture was Law spanking the hell out of me. "Ungh," I moaned, feeling my juices seep between my fingers. My teeth sank into my lower lip as I gently massaged my pussy into ecstasy. My back crashed against the door, sensing my climax peeking. My mouth slacked. "Law," I softly whimpered. "Law. Law." My breathing hitched. It was there. I was about to cum, and I knew it was gon' be stronger than anything I'd ever gotten before.

I jumped at the knock at the bathroom door. "You good?" Law asked from the other side.

"Uh, yeah. I'm getting ready for bed. I'll be out in a few."

Thanks for fucking up my orgasm.

I went on and got ready for bed. When I emerged from the bathroom, I found Law lying in bed on top of the covers with his shirt off and his back facing me. I wasn't certain if this was supposed to be some form of test or what.

"Get some rest. You got a long flight ahead of you in the morning."

I tiptoed over to the bed and gently lifted the covers then slipped underneath them. Snuggling against the pillow, I lay there with my back facing him. This was gon' be my first time sleeping in the bed with Law since we got engaged. His cologne enticed me. I wanted to nestle underneath him but felt as if that was pushing it. I should've been grateful that he was this close to me in the first place.

CHAPTER THIRTY
DASH
A COUPLE DAYS LATER, BACK IN THE STATES

"Have you seen Pops? He promised that he'd go to the football game with me," I said to Ma in the doorway of the kitchen. She was sitting at the island with a piece of toast up to her lips. It was still pretty early in the morning, and I wanted to catch Pops and remind him 'bout what we were doing for the day before he disappeared.

"Oh, honey, he left not too long ago. Said something about he got called into a last-minute meeting. Try his cell."

Pulling my phone from my pocket, I dialed Pops' number and waited for him to pick up. The call rolled over to voicemail. "That's just like him. He always promising shit and breaking promises."

"Watch your mouth. Your father is a busy man. He does whatever necessary to provide for this family."

"Is that why he promised Honey off to the mafia?"

Ma's hands slammed against the island, and she spun in her seat to face me. From the crease in her forehead, I knew she was 'bout to go in on my ass. "Says the person who put him in that predicament. Had you not been out here acting like a thug, he wouldn't have had to promise her to anybody. Would you have rather they killed us all because you wanted to be inconsiderate?"

"That's not what I was saying."

"Sounds like it to me, so the next time you want to fix your mouth and challenge something your father did for this family, think about what you did to put us in that position."

"Whatever," I said, mumbling, and stormed off.

All they ever did was try to make me the problem of the family. I tried my fucking best to do whatever I was supposed to and not step on any fucking toes. Yeah, I fucked up, and I tossed my best friend under the fucking bus to try and fix my screw up. Pops wasn't the only one out here making hard decisions for this family.

I don't know why I believed he was gon' actually spend time with me today. When I first brought the idea to him 'bout going to the game, I should've known he was lying. He never did anything any of us wanted. All he did was parade us around like we were for show.

My phone chimed. Thinking it was Pops, I quickly pulled it from my pocket just to see it was Wick texting me. Ever since he robbed the Blancos, he hadn't really been speaking to me. I wasn't certain why he was talking to me now.

Wick: *Can you meet me at our spot in thirty minutes?*

When he asked that, my first mind went to needing to tell Streets or Law that I'd heard from him since I knew they were looking for him, but I decided to give him the benefit of the doubt and go see what he wanted. I jogged upstairs and tossed on some clothes then headed straight out the front door.

It didn't take me no time to make it to Ridgecrest where we used to hoop at. Over the last few months, shit had slowed between us and we hadn't been spending much time doing the things we used to love. Wick was too focused on the dollar and trying to get it by any means necessary, instead of taking his ass out there and getting a decent paying job like a normal person. I'd never understand how come he wanted the fast cash in the first place. Just as quick as it touched his hands, the faster it'd disappear.

When I pulled into the parking lot, I found his car parked out front. Getting out, I went inside the building and found him tossing 'round a basketball. Surprisingly, he was the only one in there. Maybe he'd called me here 'cause he missed spending time with me. Immediately pulling my shirt over my head, I tossed it to the side and strolled in his direction.

"Wassup?" I said as I approached.

Wick stopped and tossed the ball into my chest. It smacked me, and I sensed the hostility behind it. "What's your problem?" I questioned him as I dribbled the ball and tossed it toward the goal. The net made a swooshing sound as the ball effortlessly went through it.

"You told Law that I was the one who robbed him?"

I swallowed hard the lump that formed in my throat. "I did what the fuck I had to do. He came there thinking that I had something to do with that shit. I was protecting my family."

"Nigga, you didn't have to tell his ass shit. You know he came by and chopped off one of Pops' fingers and threatened to chop off more if I didn't turn myself over to him? I had to get 'em out of here 'cause of you."

"And that could have been my family 'cause of you." Wick shook his head and grabbed the ball. I observed him as he bounced it.

"He could have killed them. You know that, right?"

"And I'm sorry, but I can't put my family through any more bullshit. Honey's already in a dilemma 'cause of us. What happened, that shit's on you. Before you robbed that place, you knew there could be consequences behind that shit."

"You supposed to be my best friend. Nigga, I looked at you as a fucking brother."

"When your so-called brother starts putting you in compromising positions, then you have to reevaluate some shit."

"You just don't fucking get it." He shoved the ball at me again. This time, it knocked the wind out of me when it smacked me in the chest. "All I ever wanted was to make a good life for my family. You got it made. You don't have to worry 'bout anything in the fucking world. You go to bed on a full stomach every single night. Your lights and water don't ever get cut off. You never have to worry 'bout coming home to an eviction notice on the door."

"Wick, you're standing here telling me things that I already know has been happening with you. We've been friends for forever. You also know that every chance I get, I'll do whatever I can to help you."

"That shit's not enough no more. You threw me under the fucking bus. I can't trust you no more," he said as he tread over to his bookbag that lay on the floor by the bleachers. I stood there and watched him as he picked it up from the floor and unzipped it. "I really wish shit hadn't come down to this." Reaching into the bag, he pulled out a pistol and turned in my direction. My heart stopped in my chest.

"What the fuck are you 'bout to do?" I asked him as if I didn't already know what was coming next. A part of me was hoping that I'd be able to talk him out of it. Wick knew I didn't carry a weapon on me. This nigga brought me out here to end my fucking life. I should've gone with my first mind and told the Blancos where his bitch ass was at.

"I love you, Dash." Tears filled the brims of his eyes as he glared at me. "I really hate it had to come down to this." His hand lifted in my direction.

"Wick, you really don't have to do this. C'mon, man, it's me, Dash." Moisture filled my eyes. This couldn't be how shit was gon' end for me. I was still young. I still had a lot to live for. "Please," escaped my lips.

"I'm sorry, bruh."

Pow!

My chest burned as the hot lead seeped through it. Blood began to fill my airways. I dropped to my knees and stared straight at Wick. Tears seeped down his cheeks as he took a step closer in my direction. His hand lifted toward my forehead.

"I'll always love you," were his last words as he released a single bullet, and everything went black for me.

CHAPTER THIRTY-ONE
LAW

Pops had out the blue called and asked if I could show up for dinner tonight. He was expecting me to bring Honey along. We had only been back in the states for a few hours before I received the phone call. Honey had been keeping her distance from me in her bedroom after the shit that happened back in Bali. I spanked her... she needed to know what happened when she disobeyed me. From the look in her eyes, it seemed as if she enjoyed it more than anything.

I can't lie, when that moan seeped from her lips, it took every fiber of my being not to fuck that girl. Desperation flowed through my core. The only thing that really saved her was when she got up and went into that bathroom to get ready for bed. Had she stood there a moment longer, there was no telling what would've transpired.

Getting up from the side of the bed, I headed on the opposite side of the house to let Honey know that we had plans. After the stunt she pulled, I was gon' have to keep better watch on her ass. All she did was extend her bedroom sentence.

Unlocking the door, I entered the room and found Honey

standing there with a towel wrapped around her. Her frame was still damp from the shower and her hair was wet and in its curly state. Her eyes peered at me. This girl was so fucking beautiful. God definitely knew what he was doing when he created her. Though I wouldn't dare say it out loud, it didn't stop me from admiring her.

"We're going to dinner. Get dressed."

"I'm tired. I don't feel like going anywhere."

"Did I ask you what you felt like doing? I said get dressed, and I'm not gon' tell you again," I said and left out the bedroom.

It wouldn't take me long to get dressed. All I had to do was shower and pull a suit from the closet. Heading straight into my bathroom, I stripped out my clothes and stepped over into the shower. By the time I was done handling my hygiene and getting dressed, Honey should've already been ready. She was fresh out the shower the first time I went to her bedroom, so she had no excuses.

I went back to her room and knocked on the door before opening it that time. Honey sat there at her vanity in this yellow bodycon dress. Her hair was pulled back in a bun at the nape of her neck. "I'm ready," she said and rose to her feet, grabbing her purse off the dresser. Without uttering another word to me, she brushed past me out the bedroom. My eyes temporarily shut as I took in her sweet lavender scent.

We went out the front door where Fredrick was waiting for us with the Maybach. We only brought out the foreigns for special occasions. Considering Pops never really invited us for dinner unless it was a holiday or a special occasion, I felt it was needed.

I stood there and waited for Honey to slide into the seat before getting in behind her. Fredrick shut the door behind me and got into the driver's seat. The ride started out quiet, but Honey broke the silence.

"Are we gonna talk about what happened in Bali?" Fredrick briefly glanced at me in the rearview.

"There's nothing to talk about."

Honey shifted in her seat where she was facing me. "How you gon' sit there and tell that bold face lie like that. I know you felt that connection. You're willing to just sit there and ignore it?"

"I don't connect with people."

"Why the hell not? I understand that you don't want to fall in love with a woman 'cause of what happened with your mama, but damn, you don't think you deserve to be loved? Even though I'm being forced to be here, don't you think I deserve to feel love?"

"Honey, you can always leave if it's an issue."

"No I can't, and you know that."

"I don't know what you want from me."

"I want love! I want to be treated equal! I want affection! I want to be held some nights! I want to be able to feel at home! God!" Tossing her hands up in the air, tears trickled down her cheeks. I never expected her to want any of that from me. We both were being forced into this shit. Doing the bare minimum to keep up appearances should've been enough for both of us, but I guess not.

"You can't even look me in the face." She wept softly alongside me. The car came to a stop in front of Pops' door. "Why don't y'all just take me out of my misery? I think I'd rather be dead than to keep going through this," she said and climbed out the car, leaving the door wide open behind her.

"Permission to speak, sir?" Fredrick asked as he turned to face me. I nodded and he continued. "She's right. You're being a lil too hard on her. She didn't ask to be here, but if she's willing to give it a try, why shouldn't you?"

Ignoring his question, I got out the car and went up to the front door where Honey waited for me. She'd fixed her makeup and showed no signs of asking for death a few moments prior. She cut her eyes in my direction as I unlocked the front door and gestured for her to enter the house. I led her down the hallway to the dining room where I knew everyone would've been waiting for us. When we stepped into the dining room, Streets was the only one sitting at the table with a glass of Louis XIII. I figured that's what he was drinking since it was the only thing Pops drank and supplied.

"You know why he called us here?" I asked him and pulled a chair out for Honey. She took her seat, and I pushed her up to the table.

"No clue."

"Where is he?"

"I don't know. I haven't seen him since I arrived fifteen minutes ago. I was told to wait for him in here."

Soon as I took my seat at the table, I could hear his loafers on the marble floor approaching. Streets' eyes darted over my head and his mouth dropped to the table, which was the only reason why I turned around to see what the hell was going on.

"What the hell are you doing here?" I asked Marcia as she clung to Pops' arm. I hadn't really spoken to her ever since I walked out on her ass that day. Hell, I hadn't been messing with any of 'em that I'd been fucking. To see her standing here with Pops threw me for a loop.

"Law, watch your fucking mouth. Don't speak to my woman like that."

"Woman!" Streets and I barked in unison.

"Marcia?" Honey shifted in her seat. From her facial expression, I sensed she was just as shocked as everyone else.

"You didn't tell me that you were talking to anyone, let alone their father."

"I'd been keeping it a secret. I planned on telling you when I felt ready."

"This got to be a joke, right?" I asked them.

I had just been blowing that bitch's back out and now she was standing here supposedly talking to my Pops. What the fuck. The ho was practically begging me to marry her.

"Why would I joke about something like this?"

"This really what you called us here for?" I wanted to tell him that I'd been fucking her not too long ago, but I wasn't certain how Honey was gon' take the news once it seeped from my lips. We were already in a bad place, that was just gon' make shit worse between us, so I just kept my mouth shut and planned on speaking to Pops 'bout that shit in private.

Ever since Ma's death, Pops hadn't been talking to anyone. I figured that eventually he'd get back out there in the dating market, but I damn sure didn't think it'd be with my sloppy seconds. Marcia being here with Pops just confirmed what I already knew, the bitch just wanted someone that could take care of her. She didn't give a damn who it was, and her best option would be a Blanco. She couldn't have me, so she went for the next best thing... Pops. The ho was grimy. The exact reason why she'd never have a shot with me.

"I brought you here to meet my new woman. I wanted you all to know her and know that I'm in love."

Grabbing the Louis XIII bottle, I took a huge chug from it. Pops had really lost his fucking mind. No way he was in love with that bitch that fucking fast. She had to have been doing voodoo on him or some.

"Pops, I think this is a lot for us to wrap our minds around right now," Streets replied. "All we've ever known was for you to be with Ma and now you sprang something like this on us with someone who's more than half your age."

Marcia tightly gripped Pops' hand and said, "I'm legal and that's all that should really matter." Honey got up from her seat and grabbed Marcia by the hand then disappeared. Pops took his seat at the head of the table and just sat there as if everything that was being said was soaking into his brain. I tossed back more liquor to get me through the night, knowing had I opened my mouth, it wouldn't have been anything nice to say.

"You sure 'bout this?" Streets questioned Pops.

"I like her. I don't really see what the issue is."

Now he was sounding ignorant as hell, like we weren't clearly sitting here telling him the issue. "Marcia ain't right for you," I finally spoke up since she was no longer in the room.

His dark eyes shot in my direction, and he asked, "How you figure?"

"That girl is money hungry."

"Look, Law, y'all should've known that I'd move on eventually. Just like y'all, I desire companionship too. It just so happens that it's her. As long as I'm happy should be the only thing that matters, right?"

"But what if she's after your money?"

"What makes you think that? Does she give off gold digger vibes? She seems sweet to me after the period of time of me knowing her."

"Can't you just take my word for it?"

Pops stroked his goatee as he poured himself something to drink. "And what if you're wrong 'bout her?"

Pinching the bridge of my nose, I said, "I've been fucking Marcia."

"You've been what!" Honey's voice erupted from behind me.

I shot to my feet and faced her. The innocence in her face was no longer there. It was replaced with rage. For whatever reason, I felt the need to defend myself and try to smooth out the damage I hadn't intentionally caused.

"What the fuck is he talking about?" she asked Marcia and folded her arms over her chest. Honey looked as if she was prepared to whup both of our asses. Shit, I didn't even blame her.

"Honey, I'd been fucking her before you signed the contract for us to get married. It wasn't anything serious."

"So this is why you've been acting weird toward me? You were mad that I was marrying the man you were secretly fucking?"

"How is it fair that I've been after him for months and you swoop in and steal him? I finally had something to myself and in Honey fashion, you stole it like always."

"I don't understand. You act as if we're in competition with each other or something. All I've ever done was be a friend to you. I'm sorry if you feel some type of way, but I don't be doing anything to purposely hurt you."

The waterworks began, and I called bullshit.

Facing Pops again, I said, "Now that you know the truth, you still think you're in love?"

He didn't utter another word, just got up from the table.

"When's the last time y'all had sex?" Honey asked us. Marcia's eyes locked with mine. "Has it been since we've been engaged?"

Marcia couldn't find the right words for her and waited for me to respond. She was probably terrified that Honey was gon' slap the shit out of her or even worse, drag her ass all over this house.

"Yeah, once, but that's it," I spoke up. Honey pursed her lips, nodded, and stormed out of here.

"I hope you're happy," Marcia said and ran behind Honey. I looked over at Streets and he just shrugged his shoulders. That nigga wasn't any help at all.

After waiting a moment, I went toward the front of the house in hopes that Honey had cooled down but found her outside arguing with Marcia. "I'll never fucking understand you! You were supposed to be my best friend! How could you do this to me!"

"I don't understand why you're so fucking upset when you didn't even want to marry him in the first place. You got a whole meal ticket in front of yo' face and you're willing to give that shit up. And for what? 'Cause you're holding onto the glimmer of hope that you might fall in love one day? Love ain't gon' pay ya bills, Honey. The sooner you realize that, the better."

And that was the exact thing I was tryna get Pops ass to understand—Marcia wasn't shit.

Honey's back faced me, but from the tremor in her voice, I knew she was bawling her eyes out. "What's wrong with being loved? Love is one of the most beautiful things out there. If I can have that, I'd be set for life. I don't want the fucking world, Marcia. That's what all of y'all fail to realize."

"Fine. That's yo' life. Do what you want." Marcia marched off, but she wasn't in the space to be the one angry. We both betrayed Honey. She should've been the one throwing a tantrum.

"Ugh!" Honey tossed her hands up in the air and paced alongside the car. Shoving my hands in my pockets, I approached her.

"You ready?" I smoothly asked in hopes she didn't swing on my ass.

Honey stopped and glared at me. "Is it your sole mission to

break me? You wanna damage me where I'm not capable of love or something?"

"Shit ain't even nothing like that."

"I can't tell."

"It ain't. I'll work on it."

"That's really all you got to offer me? You'll fucking work on it?"

"Shrugging, I asked, "What else you want from me?"

"Nothing, Law. Nothing," were her last words before she climbed into the car. I got in alongside her and the ride back home was a silent one.

CHAPTER THIRTY-TWO
COCO
THE FOLLOWING DAY

And Jamichael gripped her by the face, meshing their lips. The end.

For most of the day, I had been sitting in the library with a book shoved in my face and my phone on do not disturb. The escape from reality was much needed, especially after we were basically dragged from our birthday vacation. Honey told us that even though she was being forced to come back home, we could stay 'til the trip was over, but I didn't feel right staying there while she was gone, so we just came back with her. It was insane for Law to come all the way there just to get her. When she came up with that plan, that didn't cross her mind. It was cool though.

Now that we were back home, I was catching up on some much-needed reading. The book I'd been reading had caught my eye on the first page and I couldn't seem to put it down. Getting up from the bean bag I'd dove into earlier, I placed the book back on the shelf and grabbed a few others to check out and take home with me. It was going on two o'clock and I needed to get back to the world before my parents sent out a missing person report.

Exiting the library, my driver sat there in the truck waiting for me. Honestly, I never understood how they did it—sitting there in the truck doing absolutely nothing waiting for us to return to take us to our next destination. I'd go crazy if I were them.

"I'm going home," I told him as I climbed into the back and shut the door behind me.

Without uttering a word, he placed the truck in reverse and backed out his spot. I watched as the buildings and trees zoomed by on the way home. By the time we made it to the house, the gate was closed for the first time in what seemed like forever and there were several paparazzi at the gate. Their cameras began to flash soon as they noticed my truck.

"What's going on?" I asked the driver, and he shrugged.

Stopping at the gate, he punched in the code as lights flashed in his face. People began shouting at him in unison where I couldn't make out exactly what they were saying. He drove on into the fence and the door shut behind us. As we approached the house, the door opened, and Ma stepped out onto the porch. Her eyes were red and puffy. I could tell she'd been crying, but my question was why?

Without waiting for the driver, I climbed out the truck and rushed up the short steps. "What's going on?"

"How come you haven't been answering the phone?"

"It's on DND."

"I've been trying to reach you. It's Dash."

"Ma, what are you saying? Is he okay?" Tears filled the brims of my eyes because deep in my heart, I knew the answer to that question.

"He's dead, Coco."

"No." My vision blurred, and I shook my head. "No. You're lying."

"I wish I was." Tears cascaded her cheeks. "My baby is gone."

I pulled Ma into my embrace, and she broke down in my arms. We stood there on the porch, and I held her 'til she gained her composure.

"I'll be right back," I said as I trotted down the stairs.

"Where are you going?" she asked, but I ignored her question.

Jumping back into the truck, I told the driver, "Take me to Blanco's downtown." If Dash was dead, there was only one person I knew that could've pulled that trigger. If they killed my brother, I swear to God... I don't know what I'd do, but it damn sure wouldn't be anything pretty. We were getting justice for Dash, one way or another.

The driver finally arrived at the building, and I jumped from the truck before it came to a complete stop. "Is Streets here?" I asked soon as I burst through the door.

"You can't go back there!" the girl yelled at me as I marched in the direction of his office without waiting for her response.

I swung Streets' office door open, and his eyes peered over at me. "What are you doing here, Coco?" He removed himself from his seat and came over to where I stood. Before I knew it, my palm connected with his cheek. "What was that for?" he asked, soothingly rubbing his face.

"Did y'all have Dash killed? And don't fucking lie to me."

"Huh? What are you talking about?"

"Dash is dead. Did y'all kill him!"

Stepping around me, Streets shut the door and gripped me softly by the hand. He pulled me over to the leather couch in his office and eased me down on it by the shoulders. "First, we didn't kill anyone. I have no knowledge of there being a hit out on Dash, but if it makes you feel any better, I'll call Law right now and make sure."

I nodded because I needed to know. I needed to make certain that the guy who was slowly capturing my heart didn't have anything to do with my brother's death. Deep in my heart, I didn't think Streets would do anything like that to hurt me, but I didn't know what the hell his brother was capable of. Hell, his father was ready to murder us not too long ago over a stolen car.

Streets got up and grabbed his phone off his desk. My leg bounced as I waited to hear Law's voice come over the line. "Wassup?" Law answered.

Streets' eyes cut to me before asking, "Was Dash your doing?"

"Nah. I saw that shit on the news not too long ago. I was just 'bout to go to the house and check on Honey. I'on know if she knows already or not."

"A'ight, I was just making sure."

The line went dead and Streets slipped his phone into his pocket.

"If he didn't kill him, then who did?"

"I don't know, but I promise I'll find out."

Sniffling, I said, "I really can't believe he's gone."

Streets slid closer to me and draped his arm around my neck. I nestled closer to him and cried into his chest. Dash was gone, and my life was about to change forever.

CHAPTER THIRTY-THREE
LAW

I got off the phone with Streets and left out of the dealership. Dash's death had been all over the news before he called, and I wasn't surprised that someone had got his ass. The way he was living and fucking with people, he was bound to get caught soon rather than later. Wick's ass was next on the list. That lil shit was still in hiding after that shit he pulled. I even placed a price on his head. I didn't give a damn if they brought me that bitch's head, long as he was dead, that's all that really mattered.

"Take me to the house," I instructed Fredrick.

Nodding, he shut the door behind me and got into the driver's seat. There was no telling what was going through Honey's mind right now if she knew of Dash's death. She probably thought I was the one who killed him. For whatever reason, I just had to see her and make sure she was alright. Though Honey and I had our differences, she was starting to grow on a nigga. Her emotions were roping me in, and I wasn't sure how I felt 'bout that shit.

Fredrick pulled up to the house and I went inside straight

up to Honey's bedroom. I knocked once on the door and pushed it in. She wasn't in the bed, so I tried the bathroom and came up empty-handed. When I turned around, I stared down the barrel of a gun.

"It's not enough that you had to take my life away from me, but you had to take Dash's too?"

"Honey, you've been trying to kill me ever since you stepped foot in this house. If killing me gon' make you feel better..." I stepped closer to the gun where it pressed me in the throat. "Gone pull the trigger and take your life back, but before you do, I just gotta tell you that I didn't kill Dash. I don't know who killed him, but I'll dedicate my time to figuring out who did. You just gotta trust me."

Tears trailed her cheeks as she stared me in the face. Honey was bold as shit. Whether she knew it or not, she just might be exactly what I needed by my side. I saw some of me in her, and that's probably what was drawing me to her ass.

"I tried talking to Dash to keep him out of trouble, but every time I turned around, he was in some shit. Now he done got himself into some shit that took his life." Her hand lowered and mine covered the barrel of the gun. Gliding my fingertips up the gun to her hand, I eased the gun out her hand and tucked it in my waistline.

Note to self, change hiding spots.

Honey had to have been going through my shit for her to come across a gun. There was no telling what else she found in the house. I should've known her curious ass wasn't gon' listen to the rules and stay out of shit.

Honey tightly gripped me by the shirt and buried her face in my chest. My body went rigid temporarily, but I wrapped my arms around her and gave her the comfort she was seeking. After holding her for a while, she found her way over to the bed and slipped underneath the covers.

"Can you hold me?" she asked. That was a lil more intimate than I was trying to be, but who was I to turn her down in her time of need?

Stepping to the side of the bed, I kicked my shoes off and climbed in behind her on top of the covers. I spooned her from behind and she nestled back on my dick. *Please let that mufucka behave.* This was the wrong time for it to decide it wanna brick. In my defense, it had been a while since I had some pussy.

Closing my eyes, I took a whiff of Honey's strawberry-scented hair. Her frame fit mine like a puzzle piece. I'd be lying to myself if I said everything 'bout her wasn't perfect for me. Out of all the women I'd ever come across, Honey seemed to be the only one that'd be able to handle me. Dash was a pain in the fucking ass, but him stealing that car probably was the best thing that ever happened to me. I think I found my equal, but only time was gon' tell.

I held Honey 'til I heard her light snores next to me. Despite her being sleep, I didn't want to peel away from her to go downstairs and grab something to eat. My stomach was touching my mufuckin' back. Pulling my phone out, I went to Door Dash to order something to be dropped off. Not knowing much 'bout what Honey liked and disliked made it hard for me to figure out what to order.

Closing the app, I went to my messages and shot Nigel a text. He'd be the only person that was able to help me 'cause he spent so much time with her.

What does Honey like to eat?

Nigel: *Snacks or food?*

Me: *Food.*

Nigel: *She's a seafood type of girl but she enjoys a good steak too. Really, you can't go wrong feeding her. She eats about everything.*

I went back to the application and went straight to Juicy

Seafood and ordered her a seafood boil. With everything she was going through right now, I wasn't certain if she was gon' eat it, but it was worth a try.

After ordering our food, I slipped my phone back into my pocket and rested my face against her back. I couldn't even say the last time I did some shit like this. Every female I ever fucked with, I never cuddled 'em. I always dipped after sex so I wouldn't get connected to 'em. Here Honey was, making me do shit I wasn't used to without a thought in the world.

I had been laying there for so long, I dozed off. "Sir?" Nigel's voice grasped my attention. Peeling my eyes open, I saw him standing in Honey's doorway with a bag in his hand. "Your food arrived. Should I take it down to the dining room?"

"That's not necessary," I told him and slipped from underneath Honey. She stirred in her sleep and turned over, wiping her eyes with her knuckles.

"Did I doze off?"

"Yeah. I ordered us something to eat while you were sleeping." I damn sure wasn't 'bout to tell her that I was so at peace that I'd fallen asleep my damn self. So much shit had been going on lately that it was hard for me to sleep. Most nights, I tossed and turned all night long or had nightmares of me almost getting murdered. Being up under Honey calmed me. It was something I didn't even know I needed. At this point, she probably wasn't gon' be able to get rid of my ass.

"I'm not sure if you want to eat anything though, but it was worth a try," I said as I neared the bed with the bag.

"I don't have much of an appetite."

"Starving yourself isn't gon' make shit any better. Just take a bite. You don't even have to eat much." I opened the bag and handed her the food.

"This has disaster written all over it," she said and got up from the bed. I watched her as she eased down on the floor.

"I'm a messy eater. The bed would've needed to be changed by the time I was done." She snickered for the first time ever around me. It kinda caught me off guard.

"I'll just let you enjoy your food and head to my room."

"Wait, you aren't going to stay in here with me? I don't think I want to be alone right now."

"Okay." I eased down onto the floor across from her and for the next few minutes, we sat there silently eating our food.

CHAPTER THIRTY-FOUR
HONEY
DASH'S FUNERAL

Ever since I heard of Dash's death, everything's been weird. Law was a lot nicer to me, though I ain't complaining. I liked this side of him but knew it was only temporary.

This was the day I'd been dreading. I wasn't ready to lay my brother to rest. For the entire week, we'd been running around like chickens with our heads cut off trying to prepare for everything. Everywhere we turned, there were cameras flashing in our faces. Coco and I took off time from school just to have some privacy. It was insane how those people didn't think we needed time to ourselves to grieve properly.

"You ready?" Law asked from my bedroom doorway. It was weird that he was going to Dash's funeral with me, but I guess I had to get used to stuff like that. He was my fiancé after all.

"As ready as I'm gon' be," I replied and grabbed my Gucci shades and clutch off the dresser. I had every intention of sitting through the entire funeral with my shades on my face. None of those people were 'bout to be in my face. Most of them were just there to be fucking nosey and others were pretending like they actually gave a fuck about him because let's be real, if they actually did, where the fuck were they?

I followed Law out the bedroom and downstairs. We exited the house, and his driver opened the door on an Escalade for us. We climbed inside and he took us straight to the church where we were instructed to meet. I glanced at Law as he sat there scrolling on his phone. From what I'd concluded, he wasn't really a phone person unless he was handling business. He looked so fucking handsome sitting alongside me in his black suit, and don't let me get started on the way he smelled. This man made me want to lick him from the tip of his head down to his toes.

"I haven't heard anything back 'bout Dash's murder yet," he blurted, catching me by surprise.

"You're actually looking into it?"

His gaze synced with mine, and he replied, "My word is bond. If I say I'm gon' do some, I'm gon' do it."

I quickly looked away and tucked my hair back behind my ear. As much as I tried to hate this man, I couldn't. He was making it mission impossible. Over the last few days, he done an entire one eighty and I found myself drawn to him. It had to be my vulnerability, right?...

The driver pulled up to the church and there were several cars parked. There were so many people out here that there weren't any parking spaces. Lucky for us, we had reserved parking by the door. Fredrick pulled up, a guy removed a cone, and he fell in line behind the rest of our cars. Paparazzi were all over the place. One would think that they'd give us a fucking break at the funeral, but nope. The crazy thing about it was, had it been them, they'd want their privacy.

Law helped me out the truck and we entered the church where my family stood there waiting for us. Coco spread her arms and I ran into them without a second thought. For so long, it had been three of us and now it was just two. I still remembered the day that Ma and Daddy brought Dash home. Coco saw them spending so much time with him that she asked them if they could return him. Ma was so tickled, but Coco didn't find anything funny. It took her a while to get used to having him around, and now we were gon' have to get used to him no longer being here.

"Can y'all line up?" the funeral director asked, and Coco released me as we fell in line. Ma and Daddy in front of us and me between Coco and Law. No way I was about to let her walk down that aisle alone. The doors to the pulpit opened and Coco clung tightly to my arm. We stepped inside and all eyes fell on us. There were so many people inside that there wasn't any more seats. People were crowded in the back of the church. I know damn well all those people didn't know Dash and damn sure didn't love him either. Nosy bitches.

We halted once we made it to the front of the church. Ma and Daddy stood there in front of Dash's white casket. From where we stood, I heard her weeping softly. Ma held her composure at the viewing better than I thought she would. It was Coco who acting a damn fool. That was the exact reason why I wasn't about to let her see his body for the final time alone. They probably would've had to come pull her crazy ass from the casket.

Ma and Daddy stepped away from the casket and took their seats. It was our turn to go up and Coco's grip on me grew stronger. Tears coursed my cheeks as I stood there and gazed down at my lil brother. The funeral home did a damn good job with him. He looked as if he was just sleeping. They covered the bullet hole in the center of his forehead effortlessly. Leaning down, I kissed him on the forehead and whispered, "I'm gon' find out who did this to you and they gon' pay. I promise you that."

Coco gripped Dash's hand and screamed out, "Lord, why!" Grabbing her by the shoulders, I pulled her away from the casket before she started acting a complete fool. We took our seats on the front pew and Wick stepped to the casket. I looked over at Law and his jaw muscles clenched. I know it was taking everything in him to act accordingly for the funeral. They were basically showing it live per Daddy's stupid ass idea. If he wanted to do something to Wick, it was gon' have to wait 'til later.

Wick kissed Dash on the forehead and took a seat on the pew behind us. The funeral director stepped to the casket and proceeded to close it. That time, Ma was the one who screamed. Ma tried to get me or Coco to get up and say a few words about Dash, but we didn't want to. When I saw Wick get up and proceed to the podium, I figured he was her next best option.

Wick's eyes darted to Dash's casket before he began. "I never thought in a million years that I'd be standing up here today. Dash was my best friend and has been ever since we were in diapers. We used to do literally everything together. One thing 'bout Dash, he always had my back whether I was right or wrong." I wanted to get up and slap the shit out of him. Wick's stupid ass decisions was probably the reason why my brother was dead. I'd told Dash several times that he needed to stop hanging with Wick. That boy was no good and it proved me correct the night he talked my brother into stealing that car and put all of our lives in danger.

"Dash was the type of person that'll give you the shirt off his back. There were several times that he looked out for me." Wick's eyes filled with tears as he gazed out at everyone then they landed on Ma. "If I could take his place in that casket, I would. That's my nigga and he deserves justice. Dash, I promise I won't rest 'til I know what really happened to you."

Wick stepped around the podium, brought his middle and index fingers up to his lips, kissed them and pressed them against Dash's casket. On his way back to his seat, he stopped and hugged Ma and Daddy.

After Wick's speech, they sung a few songs before the pallbearers got up and got Dash's casket. We filed outside behind it and stood there, watching as they slid my brother into the back of that hearse. My heart stung. The doors shut on him and I knew that wasn't the worst of it. That real pain was gon' set in when I watched them drop him into that ground. Everything was gon' become real in that instance.

Law walked me back over to the truck and we got inside, sitting quietly, waiting for the line to move. "Wick full of shit, and I'm gon' prove it," Law blurted.

My head swiftly snapped in his direction. "What are you trying to say?"

"He the reason yo' brother in that casket."

"You sound crazy. That was his best friend."

"And you really think that shit holds weight? Blood'll put you in the ground too. Some 'bout Wick not sitting right. The way he was up there talking like he's really 'bout that fucking life."

"If he's the reason why he's in there, why would he show up at the funeral?"

"To keep up appearances so no one would suspect him. Most mufuckas show up to the funerals of the people they killed."

I sat there silently fidgeting with my fingers, trying to figure out if what Law just said was true. Why would Wick want my brother dead? He better pray to God Law was wrong because I swear, if he killed my brother or had something to do with it, I was gon' kill him my-fucking-self.

CHAPTER THIRTY-FIVE
LAW
A WEEK LATER

Things were slowly getting back to normal now that Dash's funeral was out the way. I'd been trying my best to give Honey the space she needed to grieve. I was certain it was hard losing a brother. If I lost Streets, there was no telling what I'd do. The police still had no leads 'bout what happened to Dash. All they knew was that his phone was missing and that they'd found his body on the west side of Montgomery at an abandoned house. They don't know how he got there or what he was doing there. As promised, I put my ear to the streets to try and find out what the fuck was going on. So far, I hadn't heard anything back, but I was positive that someone would get to talking soon.

"You son of a bitch," was all I heard when my office door burst open. Looking over my iMac, I saw Marcia standing there with Maya behind her.

"I'm so sorry, Mr. Blanco. I tried to stop her."

"It's fine." Getting up from my desk, I gripped Marcia roughly by the forearm and pulled her into my office, shutting the door behind her. One thing I wasn't 'bout to allow her to do was cause a fucking scene in front of clients. "Have you lost yo' fucking mind?" I slung her around where she was standing between me and my desk. She was lucky I didn't break her fucking neck for barging into my office like that.

"Yo' daddy ghosted me 'cause of you."

My brows furrowed. "I fucked up yo' pay day, so what. You're crazy as hell if you think I was just gon' stand around and watch you use him without saying anything. You wasted yo' time coming here. You might as well take yo' ass on back wherever the fuck you came from." Dismissing her, I went back 'round my desk and sat back in my chair. I had other things to worry 'bout other than her being angry 'cause she wasn't set for life like she assumed.

"Would it have killed you to let me be fucking great? You ain't want me, so I found somebody else that did."

"And you don't want him. He's just a pawn in one of yo' sick ass games. Had he not left you alone willingly, yo' ass would've disappeared. Either way, you wasn't 'bout to be a problem." Her mouth slacked.

"And how do you think Honey would've felt if I just disappeared?"

"Nothing. Absolutely nothing. At this point she can't stand yo' ass for sleeping with her fiancé."

"And you think she likes you?" Marcia's hands slammed against my desk. She eyeballed me and said, "Every chance she gets, she's down talking yo' ass. I'm the one who told her that she should be lucky to have you. That girl don't fucking want you. She wants love and you can't provide that. You don't love shit."

"Well that may be true, but we shall see, won't we?"

"I hope she runs out on yo' stupid ass and leaves you standing at that fucking altar."

"I think you got a better chance of you walking out that

door and getting hit by a bus than that ever happening. You can see yourself out." I took my attention back to my computer screen.

"We'll see, won't we?" was the last thing Marcia said before storming out my office and slamming my door behind her.

After sitting at the dealership for most of the day, it was nearing dinner time and I wanted to make it home at a decent time so that Honey didn't have to eat alone. On my way to the house, I stopped by the store and grabbed her a bouquet of simple red roses. I was far from the romantic type, but I remembered that Pops used to bring Ma flowers sometimes and it made her feel better. Maybe it'll work for Honey as well.

Entering the house, I made my way to the dining room where I figured Honey would already be. I stopped in the doorway admiring her beauty. She sat there in an oversized t-shirt and her hair was pulled up in a messy bun. Honey looked as if this was her first time climbing out of bed for the day. Soon as she felt my presence, her eyes connected with mine. The corner of her mouth quirked when she saw the flowers gripped tightly in my clutches.

Tilting her head to the side, she said, "If I remember correctly, I was told not to expect anything, especially nothing romantic. What are you doing with flowers, Mr. Blanco?"

Strolling over to her, I shoved the flowers in her direction and replied, "Take 'em before I change my mind."

Giggling, she softly removed the flowers from my grasp and took a whiff of 'em. "Thank you. They're beautiful." Nigel rushed over and grabbed 'em from her.

"I'll place them in a vase and put them in your room immediately," he said and exited the dining room.

Undoing my suit jacket, I took a seat at the head of the table. Honey silently went back to her food as if she was lost in a trance. "I wanted to see how you were doing," I interrupted her.

Her eyes shot to me, and she responded, "Wow, flowers and now therapy. Wonder what I did to deserve all this."

"I'm being serious, Honey. You just went through something traumatic. I just want to see where your head is at."

"I'm doing as good as I'm gon' do. I'll get there."

Nigel came back into the dining room with a plate for me. Before I was even able to pick the fork up and begin to eat, my phone chimed. Pulling it out my pocket, I looked down and saw it was a message from Streets.

Streets: *The Giuseppes want a meeting as soon as possible.*

And so the bullshit begins.

CHAPTER THIRTY-SIX
COCO
A COUPLE DAYS LATER

Mama Ada reached out to me and invited me to come out with her and Honey for the day. I wasn't certain what all her plans were, but she did say something about going to bingo. I'd never been to bingo before and hadn't played it since I was in like elementary school, but it did beat sitting in the house all day doing absolutely nothing.

If I was being honest, I liked hanging around her even though she was trying to push Streets off on me. Streets and I hadn't really been spending much time with each other since Dash's death. He'd been staying away as if I asked him to. The last time we were alone together was when I asked him if they had something to do with him dying. Maybe talking to Mama Ada today would help me clear up a few things.

My truck pulled into the driveway of Honey's house where Mama Ada asked me to meet her. I got out and went up to the front door. Nigel pulled it open as if he'd been standing there waiting for me to arrive. I'd never understand how he didn't go insane doing this job. I couldn't stay stuck in this house all day long, waiting on someone hand and foot. He had no life whatsoever. It was sad actually.

"Where's Honey and Mama Ada?" I asked him as I stepped into the house.

"They're in the sunroom. They've been expecting you. Right this way." I followed him down the hallway to a room that was nothing but glass. The sun shone brightly on the all-white décor. Honey and Mama Ada sat on the couch snickering as I entered the room. This was the hardest I'd seen Honey laugh ever since Dash died. Maybe it was possible to get back to ourselves... eventually.

"Hey," I spoke, and both of them looked in my direction.

"Hey." Honey continued to laugh and wipe the tears from her eyes with her fingertips. "Mama Ada was just telling me about how Law got himself stuck in a treehouse when he was little. He's afraid of heights. Imagine that." She erupted in laughter. If Mama Ada knew any better, she wouldn't have opened her mouth and told Honey that. Now she was about to hang that shit over that man's head for the rest of her life.

Mama Ada picked up a coffee mug off the coffee table and placed it to her lips. "You have any funny stories about Streets?" Honey's eyes cut in my direction, and she tooted her lips. It was no secret that I liked him. What was the point in hiding it? Streets was an extremely attractive man with a good head on his shoulders and treated me well.

"Sit. Sit." Mama Ada patted the empty seat alongside her. "I have stories for days about both of my boys."

"I can't wait to hear this." I giggled as I waited for Mama Ada to get to talking about Streets.

"One time Streets called himself waiting 'til everyone went to bed and stole one of the cars out the driveway when he was ten. That boy rode around for hours 'til he ended up crashing it and having to walk back home. The next morning when everyone was looking for the car, he pretended like he didn't know anything about it missing 'til someone called and said they found it totaled. That boy had totaled it at the gaming store. They whupped his tail so good, he never stole anything else."

"Wait, so how'd they know it was him that wrecked it?" I quickly questioned.

"His stupid self crashed right in front of the camera. They had his big-headed ass on video climbing out and staggering."

Honey erupted in laughter.

"Man, wait 'til I see him." I laughed.

"I think that's enough storytelling for now. Are y'all ready to win some money at this bingo?" Mama Ada asked as she lifted from the couch. Nigel rushed over to clean the table before we even got fully out the way.

"Is bingo fun to you?" Honey questioned as we headed down the hallway toward the door.

"Girl, if bingo wasn't fun, I wouldn't even be going. I stay whupping ass up in there."

"It gotta be something if you're always going 'cause I know you don't need the money," I added. This was gon' be my first time going to a bingo hall. If it was anything like it was on television, the shit was gon' be boring as hell.

The driver opened the back door on the Escalade for us and we got inside. Mama Ada counted her cash while Honey scrolled social media. I sat back quietly gazing out the window on the drive to the bingo place. Streets has been on my mind heavily lately. We texted each other here and there, but we hadn't really spent any time together for real.

The truck pulled into the parking lot of Winner Bingo. The driver opened the door for us and helped Mama Ada out. My eyes scanned the parking lot and I saw some of the people that were entering. One guy wore a fresh black Nike sweat suit with a rope chain around his neck. He was every bit of seventy, but he was fresh as hell. This other woman rolled a suitcase behind her into the building. *What the hell is in there?*

We followed Mama Ada up to the entrance. When we got inside, she collected everything she needed, and we found our seats. "Look at her ugly ass," Mama Ada said with her eyes glued on this woman sitting in the corner of the room. She was older, probably had Ada by a couple years. From what I could see, she wore this ugly ass floral dress that looked like she snatched it off a couch in the seventies.

"Why you talking about that lady like that?" Honey asked her.

"That ho don't like me 'cause her boyfriend Ray always flirting with me."

"Mama Ada got a mouth on her," Honey joked.

"I'm telling the truth. She's always picking."

"She better not come picking today or else I'm gon' beat her old ass," Honey made known.

The bingo game began. Mama Ada was halfway through her board when this older gentleman stopped at the table. He was dressed in a black button down and slacks.

"You're looking good today, Ada." When those words seeped from his lips, I sensed this was Ray. I glanced over at the woman Mama Ada was talking about earlier. Two other women sat at the table with her now. They laughed and held conversation while the game continued in the background.

"Ray, why don't you take your tail on somewhere. You're always starting shit." Mama Ada waved him off, but that didn't make him leave her table. It was as if her rejection caused him to want her even more.

"I don't be starting nothing. Why don't you stop being so stubborn and go out with me sometime?"

"Ray, we both know that you're already spoken for."

"Who? Me?" Laughing, he poked himself in the chest with his index finger. "Lilith and I aren't together anymore."

"You know you can lie." Mama Ada shook her head. "I'm not about to play with you."

"Ray Allen!" a female's voice yelled. When I looked up, the woman Mama Ada was talking about was approaching our table with her friends directly on her track. Ray wasn't even the best looking guy in here, which was probably why Ada wasn't feeding into his bullshit.

"See, always starting shit," Mama Ada said, mumbling.

"Lilith, why don't you take yo' ass on back over yonder." Ray turned back to face Mama Ada and she rolled her eyes.

"Why don't you gone before she gets over here? You know how much I can't stand that bitch."

"Filthy mouth," Honey joked and laughed. We were definitely seeing a different side of Ada. Bingo brought out the worst in her.

"What I told you 'bout messing with my man?" Lilith stopped at our table and asked.

"Lilith, as you can fucking see, I'm not messing with his ass. If anything, I'm begging him to leave me the hell alone. Why don't you take him on back to the table with you?"

"C'mon y'all. It's enough of Ray to go around."

See, now he was pissing me the fuck off, trying to play in her face and shit. Scum bag.

"In your fucking dreams, Ray."

"You don't wanna know what be happening in my dreams." Ray winked at her and I almost vomited in my mouth.

"Ray, can't you see that she doesn't want to be bothered with y'all? Can y'all get the fuck away from our table?" Honey stepped in just like I knew she would, eventually.

"Lil girl, I don't know who you think you're talking to,"

Lilith said with her hand resting on her hip. "Ada needs to get her cheating ass up outta here. She comes in here all the time cheating and ruining the fun for everybody else."

"I got your lil girl." Honey rose from her seat but I pulled her back down.

"You can't cheat in bingo, Lilith. If you were smart, you'd know that. I be winning fair and square. Not my fault you sorry. Now take ya man and get away from my fucking table."

"Why you gotta be so mean?" Ray asked her and took a seat next to her. Mama Ada's body went rigid. She was uncomfortable and I could tell.

"Let me go," Honey said underneath her breath. I released the fool and she jumped to her feet.

Lilith reached across and yanked all Mama Ada's stuff to the floor. Ada bolted to her feet, balled her small hands into fists, and before I knew it, one of them connected with Lilith's jaw. She hit her so hard that her nappy ass bob wig turned sideways.

"C'mon, y'all really don't have to fight over me." Ray was stupid as hell if he thought Ada was fighting over him. It was the disrespect.

Lilith clutched her face and her mouth slacked as she peered at Ada. "I asked y'all nicely to leave my table. All I wanted was to play bingo in peace."

"See, now I gotta whup yo' ass," Lilith said. She swung at Ada and missed. Ada shoved her to the floor, sat down on her, and sent blow after blow to her face. The way Ada was whupping her ass, one wouldn't even think she was elderly.

Lilith's friends began to close in as if they thought their old asses were gon' jump Ada or something. Honey jumped straight in their way, snatched one of their canes from them, and tripped both of them to the floor. "If I was y'all, I'd stay down there," she warned.

The security rushed over and pulled Ada off Lilith. He held her back as she kicked her lil legs. "Let me go!" Ada shouted.

"Put her down, with yo' ugly ass," Honey said, swinging the cane as if she was about to use it on his ass next.

"I want to press charges. She attacked me," Lilith spoke from the floor. Ada had knocked her damn dentures out her mouth. She picked them up and slipped them back in before Ray helped her from the floor.

"I wish you fucking would. You came over here messing with me," Ada replied. The security finally placed her back on her feet but behind him where she couldn't reach Lilith.

"You're more than welcome to press charges if you want, but you'd have to do that outside because they have to leave. You're banned from the bingo hall, Ada. There's a strict no fighting policy."

"You'll be hearing from my son," Ada told him and began to gather her things along with my help. Hearing her say that, I knew that wasn't good for anybody. There was no telling what he was gon' do to their asses once he knew that Ada was upset.

He escorted us out of the building and Ada wasted no time getting on the phone to call her son. "I can't believe you were actually about to fight those old people," I told Honey as we walked to the truck.

"You wanted me to let them jump her? You sound crazy. I was gon' beat the dust out their asses. I'on give a fuck."

We climbed into the truck and Ada got off the phone with a huge smile on her face. "He said that he'll handle it." It was crazy that with one phone call, all her problems went away. That was the life Honey was really about to live.

CHAPTER THIRTY-SEVEN
STREETS
A FEW DAYS LATER

It had been a minute since I hung with Coco. I'd been super busy, and I wanted to catch up with her. Let her know that she'd been on my mind and I hadn't disappeared on her. It was lunchtime, so I decided to go by Chipotle and grab her some lunch then bring it to her at school. According to her schedule, she was gon' be there another few hours. Yes, I called the school, pulled some strings and got Coco's schedule. It sounded stalkerish, but I promise it was anything but.

As I climbed out the truck, I grabbed the food off the seat and checked my phone for the time. Her class ended ten minutes ago, so I headed down the sidewalk toward the building where her next class was gon' take place in hopes that I'd find her. If she wasn't there, then the cafeteria was my next step.

I approached her building and saw her sitting outside at one of the tables with a book shoved up to her face. The closer I got to her, I saw this guy stop and approach. Coco ignored him, continuing to read her book as he said something to her. She slid her book down briefly and her lips moved. He frowned and took a seat across from her. My teeth clenched. Clearly, he wasn't getting the memo to leave her the fuck alone.

I marched on in that direction and finally came into earshot. "Why you being so damn stuck up? I'm just trying to get to know you." He moved to the seat next to her and her body tensed. His hand eased over onto her thigh and mine went to my piece in my waistline. Taking a deep breath, I removed my hand, remembering where I was and that I didn't want to cause a scandal for my family to have to clean up.

Coco politely removed his hand from her and stood to her feet. "It's not polite to touch people you don't even know, especially without their consent. I should call the police on you while you're up here harassing people."

"That's not necessary," I spoke as I closed in on them. Placing the food down on the table, I stepped to dude. He was a couple inches taller than me, but I wasn't 'bout to back down. "I'm pretty sure she already let it be known that she didn't want to be bothered with you, but you couldn't take the fucking hint."

"Who the fuck are you supposed to be, nigga?" He chuckled as he eyeballed me.

"Her nigga," I answered, mugging him straight back.

"Uh," escaped Coco's lips.

"You sure got a sweet piece of ass right here."

My jaw muscles clenched and my hands balled into fists.

Wham!

I punched his ass so hard he stumbled back a bit. Hearing him talk 'bout Coco like that just did something to me.

Wham!

I uppercut his ass and he flew back into the grass. My mind went back to when I saw him putting his hand where it didn't belong.

Wham!

I kicked the shit out of his ribs and hovered the nigga. Blow after blow, I just couldn't stop punching him.

"Streets! That's enough!" Coco shouted and tugged on my forearm. "Get up. Let him go before someone calls the police!" Coco should've known by now that the police didn't put any fear in my heart. This bastard needed to learn a fucking lesson. If he was putting his hands on her, there was no telling how many other women he'd done that shit to.

"Learn to keep yo' fucking hands to yourself." I straightened my posture and the nigga rolled around on the ground, groaning. Bet he'd think twice before disrespecting another female.

Coco pulled me over to the table where she was sitting prior. She lifted my hand up to her face and studied my bruised knuckles. "I'm glad that you're taking up for me and all, but you're gonna get yourself in trouble. Look at your hands." Her lips pressed gently against my knuckles. Coco's gaze synced with mine, and she asked, "So about you being my nigga?" and snickered. "Did you really mean that?"

"You think I'm just talking for my health?" My brow arched as I gaped back at her.

"So you really want to be my boyfriend? Even though you know I'm saving myself for marriage? Do you really think you can be celibate like that?"

"Babe, I told you I'on want none of that fake ass love. If waiting to make love to you means that I get to keep you for life, then I'm down. Sex ain't shit. I want to connect with you on a deeper level. When we get to the sex part, it'll mean more for both of us."

Her eyes searched mine. "You don't feel real, you know that?"

"I'm realer than they come. You gon' eat your lunch before it gets super cold?"

"The way you're out here whupping ass, I'm sure it's already cold." She laughed and it was one of the best melodies I'd ever heard. I looked down and old dude was no longer on the ground. I hadn't even noticed when he got up.

For the rest of lunch, Coco and I sat there and ate our food. It was slightly cold, but neither of us gave a fuck. We were enjoying each other's company, the same way we always did whenever we were 'round each other.

Once we were done eating, I tossed the trash and walked her to her next class. Coco clung to my arm as we strolled down the sidewalk. Her bookbag draped over my shoulder. A few chicks eyed us but didn't utter a word. A lot of people knew who I was just by looking at me. Others knew me from hearing my name. To see Coco attached to someone of my caliber must've been shocking.

"This is me," she said and peeled away from me. Gripping her by the waist, I pulled her back into my frame 'cause I wasn't ready to let her go just yet. Coco soothed me whenever I was near her. She brought a sense of tranquility into my life that I never knew I needed.

"If I could, I'd go right in there with you. Promise I don't wanna let you go right now." My hug grew stronger.

"It's nice being up under you." Coco released a moan and squeezed me. "But I have to get to class. I can't be late or else Professor Letterman will rip me a new asshole.

"It's fine. You can just hit me up whenever you're done with yo' classes for the day."

"What are you about to do?" she questioned as I handed her the bookbag.

My phone chimed and I pulled it from my pocket. It was a text from Law.

Meet me at Winner Bingo now.

Slipping my phone back into my pocket, I cupped her face and pressed my lips firmly against the center of her forehead. "I have to go take care of some business."

I pulled up to Winner Bingo and Law's truck was already parked out front. He climbed out the back seat when he saw my vehicle come to a halt.

"What are we doing here? Mama Ada doesn't play bingo on Thursdays."

"Pops want us to teach their asses a lesson."

"What happened?"

"They banned her from coming here 'cause some old bitch was picking with her. You know Mama A got a temp. It don't take much to turn her from the loving, sweet baker to ass kicker."

"You're right 'bout that." It still amazed me how she flipped that switch. She'd be sweet then beat the hell out of you and go right back to being sweet again. That woman had a gift for sure.

Law and I entered the building. There were a few people in there playing bingo. He stopped at the desk and said, "I need to speak with the manager or the owner."

"Is it anything that I can help you with?" the chick asked him.

"No, just get the manager or fucking owner."

Her eyes expanded and she jumped to her feet. "One moment," she told him and scattered out of there. A few moments later, she came back with some white guy. He stopped in front of Law and shoved his hands into his pockets.

"Can I help you?"

"I'm here to see one of your security guards 'bout a situation that took place the other day," Law stated.

"I'm not sure what situation you're pertaining to."

"The one where he put his hands on my fucking grandma."

His eyes scanned our surroundings and he said, "Can we discuss this in the office? I don't want to disturb the customers." Law nodded and we both followed him to his office. He shut the door behind us and took a seat at his small ass metal desk. "I'm not sure what incident you're speaking of but I can ask around to see what's going on."

"That nigga put his hands on her then had the fucking nerves to tell her that she's banned from here when she didn't even start the fucking fight."

"Hhmm. Let me get someone on the phone." He hit Law with his index finger and picked his cell phone up off the desk. "Excuse me," he said and exited the office. The way shit was going, I could already sense shit wasn't gon' end good.

"What the fuck is taking him so fucking long?" Law grew impatient. If he didn't come back in here with some news soon, he was gon' take matters into his own hands.

A few moments later, the door opened, and he stepped back in the office with some black guy behind him. "I think this is the guy that was working that day."

"I need to holler at you outside," Law said as he brushed past him out the office.

"For what?"

I shoved him in the direction behind Law, and he mugged me. "Just fucking walk," I instructed him.

When we got outside, Law walked us around the back of the building out of view. He pulled his suit jacket off and gently laid it over one of the boxes and began to roll his sleeves up. "Normally, I don't like to get my hands dirty, but this is personal, not business."

"What the hell are you talking 'bout?" the guy quickly asked him.

"You put yo' fucking hands on my grandma. You don't ever disrespect her like that."

"If you're talking about that fight I broke up, all I did was grab her off the other woman before she drew blood."

"Well, yeah, I'm 'bout to draw blood from yo' ass now." Law swung on him, and his fist connected with his nose. The shit instantly leaked. Law never really liked getting into fights 'cause when we were teenagers, Ma placed him in boxing classes to displace his anger. In other words, his hands were lethal.

"Are you fucking crazy! You're out here trying to fight me for doing my fucking job."

"I don't give a fuck." Law swung on him again. This time, he split his upper lip. "Maybe next time you'll learn to keep ya fucking hands to yourself." I stood there, watching Law go blow for blow on this nigga. He swung back on him a couple times but none of 'em stuck.

Once Law was done beating his ass, he grabbed his jacket and strolled toward the front of the building. To my understanding, he was done and was 'bout to leave, but this fool went back into the building to the office.

"Back so soon?" the guy asked us when we stepped into the door.

"Y'all 'bout to shut this shit down. If my grandma ain't allowed to play here, nobody is gon' play here."

"Excuse me?" His brow arched to his hairline.

"Don't stand there and pretend like you didn't hear me fucking talking to you. Shut this shit down. You got twenty-four hours."

"I'll do no such thing," he protested.

"Then I guess I'll have no other choice but to do it for you."

"Can you leave my office before I call the cops?"

"Call 'em. I'on see what good it's gon' do you to do it though." Law pulled out his phone and his fingers swiftly moved across the keyboard. I wasn't certain what he was up to, but I was sure it wasn't anything good. "Let's go," he said to me as he brushed past me out the office.

When we got outside, he lingered around for a bit with his phone still shoved in his face. A few moments later, two black Chargers entered the parking lot. Once I saw Cortez step out the car, I knew shit was 'bout to go down. The only time he was called was when he was able to act a complete, utter fool. This bingo place wasn't gon' be stable once they walked out of there.

"Shut this shit down," Law instructed him, and he nodded. We both climbed into our trucks and got the hell out of there.

CHAPTER THIRTY-EIGHT
HONEY
A WEEK LATER

My nerves were all over the place the quicker the day came for me to marry Law. At least for my sake, he was doing much better than he was before. We'd been spending more time with each other and I was conflicted on how to feel about him now. I wasn't certain if it was Dash's death or what that drew us together, but I wasn't about to complain.

My phone chimed, alerting me that I had a reminder for an event in my calendar. It was dress fitting day. Mama Ada picked out this local dress maker to make my gown and I was nervous as hell to see what it actually looked like. He also made the maid of honor dress for Coco. After I found out that Marcia had been sleeping with Law, I called and got her dress canceled. There was no way she was about to be in my wedding and had been fucking the groom behind my back.

After that incident, she reached out and tried talking to me, but I didn't want to hear anything she had to say. Marcia was full of shit and envious as hell. It was good I saw her true colors now rather than further down the line.

Getting up from bed, I went into the bathroom to handle my hygiene so I could get ready to go. The last thing I wanted was to be late and for the dress maker to think that I didn't respect his time.

Once I was dressed, I went downstairs where I saw Mama Ada sitting there on the couch. She hadn't made it known that she was coming along for the fitting. I knew my mama was supposed to meet me there. Even though this was a wedding that I hadn't planned, this was something that she was supposed to do with me.

I'd always imagined how my wedding was gon' be, hence Coco and I making our pact to remain celibate 'til we were married. We'd sit down for hours and talk about our wedding dresses and the themes. When the wedding planner started planning, I didn't want to tell her my ideas because that was supposed to be shared with the person I love. I just agreed to everything they wanted to get it over with. Now that I thought about it, it was probably a mistake. I'd more than likely never get married again after this and missed the opportunity to plan my wedding. All I could do was pray that it's not bullshit.

"Hey," I spoke, making my presence known. Her face was buried in her phone, so she didn't see me when I came down.

"Have you seen the news?" Mama Ada asked with a smirk.

"No. What happened?"

"Come here." She patted the empty space alongside her on the couch and I slowly approached. My heart thumped against my ribcage, not knowing what she was about to tell me. It couldn't be anything terrible if she was smiling with anticipation.

When I sat down, she handed me her phone and I saw a WSFA news article about how the bingo hall burned to the ground. "Who?" My gaze met hers. That was the only thing that could seep from my lips.

"I told you that they'd handle it."

"I'd hate to get on their bad side," I said and handed her the phone back.

"You ready to go see this gorgeous dress?"

"I'm nervous," I made known.

"It's okay to be nervous. It's getting close to your big day. A lot of people get cold feet."

"If I'm being honest, I'm not sure how to feel. I kinda like Law, but I'm scared he's gon' fuck it up and go back to the old him."

"That's understandable, but someone like him, you have to give time. He needs time to navigate through his feelings. I'm sure deep down, he just wants to be loved like everyone else, he's just scared. If you don't want him to shut down on you again, you have to show him that he can trust you. That you're not going anywhere. It's not gon' be easy, but that's what you're going to have to do."

"I guess I can try that."

"Let's go before we be late." Mama Ada got up from the couch and I followed her out the door. Our driver took to us to the dress shop. When we arrived, Ma was already there waiting inside for me. My heart thumped as I climbed out the truck and went inside. Her and Coco sat on the couch sipping champagne, waiting for me to arrive.

"Hey." I embraced each of them.

"I'm so excited to see your dress," Ma quickly spoke. She'd been excited about everything when it came to the wedding for someone who didn't seem to want me to get married off in the first place.

"Honey, babe, I can't wait 'til you see the final results," Andrew said as he approached me with open arms. Andrew had been nothing short of amazing ever since I first met him. It was crazy how the Blancos knew someone in the city that did anything you can imagine.

Bouncing on my tippy toes, I said, "I'm so excited."

The door chimed and when I turned around, I saw Marcia prance inside. "What are you doing here?" Coco wasted no time asking her. Neither one of us had been hanging out with her, so I wasn't sure why she thought it was fine for her to just show up here. Common sense should've told her that she was no longer a part of the wedding.

"I had it marked on the calendar."

"Are you crazy or are you stupid? You have no reason to be here. I been canceled that dress for you," I told her and turned around because I had nothing else to say to her ass.

"Honey, are you really gon' act like that with me?"

"Tuh..." Turning, I faced her again and continued, "You're lucky this all I'm doing after finding out you've been fucking my fiancé."

"I've known you far longer than him. How can you forgive him, but not me?"

"'Cause you should've known fucking better. You were supposed to be my best friend. You were supposed to be real with me and let me know what was going on. Instead, you had me walking 'round here looking stupid. I can't be friends with someone like you."

"How 'bout I make up for it now? I really don't think you should marry Law."

"Lil girl, I really think it's time for you to leave," Mama Ada spoke up.

Gripping Marcia by the forearm, I dragged her out the door before Ada whupped her ass the same as she did Lilith.

"You really have lost your fucking mind."

"Honey, who are you fooling? We both know that you don't want to marry Law. I came to offer you a way out."

"There's no way out. I signed the contract."

"But there is. I know a guy who makes fake IDs and another that can get you out the city undetected. You can go out there and live your life how you see fit. You don't have to marry that man if you really don't want to. We both know that you want love and Law can't provide that for you."

Those were her words, but Law had been changing lately. No one changed overnight. Maybe if I gave him some time, I could grow to love him. I'd already been feeling mixed emotions about him. Then again, I could be living a fairytale and he didn't change at all. Shit.

"I can't do something like that and leave my family behind. There's no telling what they'd do if I don't marry Law, and I'm not finna let them force Coco into doing it."

"Newsflash, Streets already got that on lock. There's no way she's walking down the aisle and marrying Law. For once, you need to be thinking about yourself. Dash didn't get to live his life, but you have another chance to."

Now why the fuck did she have to bring him into this? Not a day went by that I didn't think about my brother. I've caught myself several times wanting to pick up the phone and call him just to hear his voice. I missed the fuck out of him. Lord knows I do.

"Honey, he has another client coming in an hour. You need to get in here and try on this dress," Ma said from the doorway.

"I'm coming," I tossed over my shoulder.

"Just think about it, Honey. If you change your mind, you know how to reach me," Marcia said and went to her car.

I went back into the building and Coco grabbed me before I was able to make it far. "What did she want?"

"Nothing. Just still talking about the same mess," I lied, not wanting to really tell her what Marcia had just said to me. "I'm ready," I told Andrew.

"Right this way." He led me to the back room and my mouth touched the floor when I saw my dress sitting there. I knew it was mine because he'd captured my vision to the tee. This man ate and left no crumbs. The dress was absolutely stunning.

Ever since I could remember, I'd always wanted to look like a princess on my wedding day. That was one thing I'd told Andrew when he asked me what I envisioned myself wearing. I'd fucked up and had no real say so in everything else about the wedding, but what I was putting on was all me.

The white puffy dress with white beaded lace and a long trail. That was my dream dress, and I was about to wear it in a couple weeks. A couple weeks... it was mind blowing to know that the wedding had come so quickly.

"Are you ready to try it on?" Andrew asked me as he stepped to the mannequin and unzipped the dress from behind.

I stripped out of my clothes all the way down to my bra and panties. The deep v in the dress, I wasn't supposed to wear a bra with it, but I damn sure wasn't about to display myself to Andrew even though he liked the same meat as me. I wasn't that open.

Andrew helped me into the dress and escorted me out of the room. The train on the back of the dress was so long, I was terrified that someone might step on it while I was walking. As I stepped back into the front lobby where everyone was sitting and waiting for me, everyone began to coo.

"Oh, Honey..." Ma clasped her hands together and pressed them to her lips. "You look so beautiful. I can't believe my baby girl is about to get married."

"Honey, you're gorgeous," Coco added. Looking over at Mama Ada, she wiped her eyes with her fingertips.

"If only you knew how long I've been waiting for this day."

Getting up from her seat, she approached me from behind as I stood there in the mirror gawking at myself. Her head poked from around me with a wide grin on her face. "It may have been under certain circumstances, but I really glad you were brought into my life. I can't wait 'til you're officially my grandbaby." Mama Ada pecked me gently on the cheek and went back over to her seat.

I stood there, taken aback by my own appearance. My fingertips slowly coursed the beads that lined my abdomen. This was real.

"Do you like it?" Andrew asked me, snapping me from my thoughts.

My head whipped in his direction, and I replied, "I love it. Thank you so much for grasping my vision."

"It was a pleasure working with you."

"Are you done working on my dress?" Coco questioned him. I was so wrapped up in my own dress that I'd forgotten to even ask him about hers.

"I have a few more finishing touches and it'll be done. I'll call soon as I'm done with it so that I can make sure it fits."

"Okay."

I went back and changed out the dress. Andrew placed it in a dress bag and said, "I'll make sure it's delivered before the end of the day." The dress was so huge, there was no way it was fitting in the truck with us.

When we exited the building Ma and Coco pulled me into an embrace then we parted ways. Mama Ada and I went back to the house.

"I'm going to head on home," Mama Ada said when the driver opened the back door for me. Gripping me by the arm, she pulled me into her embrace. "You're going to make a beautiful bride." Her lips pressed against my cheek, and she released me.

Climbing out the truck, I went up to the front door. Nigel pulled it open before I fully reached it. "Is he here?" I asked him. Law had been on my mind for the longest.

Nigel nodded and replied, "He's downstairs in the basement."

"The basement?" My brows furrowed. Shit, I didn't even know we had a basement.

"Yes. Want me to take you to him?"

"Okay."

I could've easily retired to my room for the evening, but for whatever reason, I needed to see him. Following Nigel to the staircase that led to the basement, we entered and took the stairs down. My feet touched the last stair, and I froze. There he was, standing there with no shirt on in nothing but his boxer briefs, and they cupped his small ass perfectly. *Wonder what the front looks like.*

My eyes trailed up his sweaty abs to his face. In one swift motion, Law punched the shit out of the black punching bag in front of him, making it slide into the wall. I stood there, stuck in a trance, admiring the hell out of him as he boxed that bag like a pro.

"Where he learned to do all that?" I whispered to Nigel. Law's head snapped in our direction. He picked up the towel off the bench next to him and wiped his face with it.

"I'll leave you to it," Nigel quickly said and jetted back up to the main floor as if he wasn't supposed to be down here.

"Where'd you learn how to do that?" I asked him as I closed the gap between us. Even him sweaty smelled divine. My pussy tingled. I wanted to lick every drop of sweat off this man; that alone let me know that I needed to get the hell from down here.

"Something I picked up as a teenager. How was the dress fitting?"

"How you know about that?"

"I know every move you make."

"I don't know if that's supposed to be comforting or what, but it was fine." Taking a seat on the bench, I sighed. "I can't believe that we're about to be married." Law didn't utter a word, just grabbed his Versace house coat and draped it over his shoulders. I hated whenever he shut down like that. Thoughts of what Marcia said to me earlier seeped back into my mind.

"You sure this is what you really want?" I asked him and stood to my feet. Law's face was mere inches away from mine. His dark eyes bored into mine, sending vibrations to my heart. My fingertips tingled to trace his face.

"What other choice do we have?" was the only thing that escaped his lips before he stepped around me and went upstairs.

CHAPTER THIRTY-NINE
LAW
A COUPLE DAYS LATER

Since our wedding day was right around the corner, I felt the need to do something nice for Honey. She deserved it. I called up my assistant and had her plan an entire date for us and tossed her something hefty to do it too. With me having commitment issues, I'd never been on a date let alone planned one. It was a first time for everything.

Honey has been in class most of the day and by the time she arrived home, I was gon' have everything set up for her. She's supposed to get pampered before taking a shower and getting dressed. Someone was paid to do her nails and makeup. A dress and pair of shoes were delivered for the evening. Everything was planned out to the letter.

As she got ready, I paced my bedroom floor, playing out in my head exactly how this night was gon' go. Everything had to be perfect. This was supposed to be a night for her to remember, there was no room for fuck ups.

Pulling my phone out my pocket, I dialed Maya's number. She answered on the second ring. "Yes, Mr. Blanco?"

"I was just calling to make sure everything was ready for the evening."

"Of course. They're just waiting for you all to arrive. Everything should be smooth sailing."

"Okay."

Ending the call, I went downstairs to the bar to grab me something to drink while I waited for her. It was taking Honey a bit longer than I anticipated to get dressed. Pouring a shot of Louis XIII, I immediately tossed it back and poured another. It took Honey a good twenty minutes before I saw the people I'd hired coming downstairs. Moments later, she descended the staircase in this velvet green mermaid dress. Her hair was in this updo with diamond accents. My eyes were drawn to her, stuck in a trance. My heart skipped numerous beats for the first time ever. It was Honey, I knew it in my bones that I was making the right decision to marry her. That's why I was trying my hardest not to shut down on her anymore. I needed to be near her at night like the air I breathe. Whenever I slept in the same bed with her, the room even, I got a full night of sleep. The nights I forced myself to stay away, I tossed and turned all night long like a rotisserie chicken.

"At a loss for words?" she asked, and the corner of her mouth quirked when she stopped directly in front of me. My fingertips had a mind of their own. They lined her collarbone up around her neck, stopping briefly before making their way to her jaw line. My thumb gently stroked her lips, and her eyes shut. "Mmhmm," escaped her lips, and my dick throbbed.

Wrapping my hand tightly around her neck, I yanked her into my frame, and her eyes shot open. "I be trying so hard to push you away."

"You don't have to. Just let me in." Her glossy eyes searched mine. I couldn't help myself, I meshed our lips, shoving my tongue into her mouth, exploring every depth of her. We kissed 'til our lips grew sore, and we were breathless. Peeling away from each other, I gripped her by the hand and led her out the door where the Maybach was waiting for us. The driver opened the door and we climbed inside.

I rented out a floor in the RSA tower to have dinner out on the balcony and overlook the Montgomery skyline. That should've been something she'd appreciate. Me taking her out probably was a shocker after the lil speech I gave her when she first moved in.

Honey faced me and asked, "Do you mind if I take a picture? I just want to remember the night." I nodded and she nestled closer to me, whipping her phone out. She snapped a picture of us, giving nothing but face like a model. Honestly, if Honey really wanted to, she could have a thriving career as a model, and I ain't talking 'bout one of those Instagram models either.

The driver pulled up to the building and opened the door for us. I got out first then helped her. She didn't ask any questions, just followed me into the building to the elevator. We went up and soon as the doors opened, we were greeted with candles and rose petals leading the way to the balcony.

"Thought you weren't the romantic type?" Honey joked when she saw the decorations. I wasn't certain what anything looked like, I just let Maya do her thing and trusted her. Maybe that was why butterflies swam in my stomach.

"I'm not. I hired someone to do it," I told her as I led her down the candlelit trail.

"Well, you get an A for effort. Most people wouldn't have even done that."

When we got out to the balcony, there was a circular table sitting out there with a black tablecloth. A small red and black balloon arch sat behind it with bouquets of red and black roses. I pulled the chair out for Honey, and she took her seat, then I sat down across from her. Our food was already on the table underneath a tray. She lifted it and her eyes lit up when she saw the lobster tail and fish. Knowing that seafood was her favorite food, I had to choose that for our meal for the evening.

"You did a good job, Mr. Blanco," she said as she picked up her fork and began to dive into her food. I did the same. We sat there silently eating our food. By the time we were done eating, Honey got up from the table and made her way over to the railing. "This is a beautiful view. You wouldn't even think that Montgomery looks like this."

Getting up, I stepped behind her. The wind lightly blew her scent up my nostrils. I closed the gap between us, pressing her ass into my pelvis. Her body went rigid at first, but eventually melted into mine. Spinning to face me, she said, "I really don't want this night to end." I stroked the loose strands of hair back out her face. She studied my face and said, "I'm beginning to fall for you. How is that even possible?"

Not having the answer to her question, my hands found her ribs, gliding up and down her velvety dress. My forehead pinned against hers. Honey's breathing labored. Her nose gently stroked mine. Our lips found each other's for the second time tonight.

Honey's fingertips tickled my ribs as they glided to my back. My dick began to brick. Gripping her by the shoulders, I softly pushed her back from me. "I haven't had sex in so long, and you're really tempting me right now. Let me get you home."

CHAPTER FORTY
COCO
THE BACHELORETTE PARTY

For weeks, I sat there and tried to figure out what to do for Honey's bachelorette party. Since I was the maid of honor, it was my duty to plan it. Had Marcia not fucked up the way she had, I would've let her take on the responsibility. It was just two of us in the wedding party, me and the bride. We didn't hang with people for real unless we were partying, so I decided that quiet time at home with Ma and Mama Ada would be the best way to end Honey's single life. Surrounded by the people she loved. Of course, we were gon' have games, food, and drinks, but for the most part, we weren't going out and getting wasted.

For the entire day, I had been running around trying to make sure that everything was decorated while Ma kept Honey busy. She just thought that she was spending the day with Ma, but we were gon' surprise her once she made it home. Law agreed to stay away for the night and stay at a hotel after his bachelor party to give us space. If I was being honest, he seemed a bit nervous about tomorrow himself.

"That sign is a bit crooked," Mama Ada said from behind me.

"It is?" I glanced her over my shoulder. She sat there on the couch with a champagne flute in her hand. By the time Honey made it here, she was gon' be good and drunk.

"Yeah, just lift it a few inches." I did as she told me and she said, "Perfect."

Stepping down from the step ladder, I took a few strides backward to admire my work. "Did you pick your dress up from the shop yet?" Mama Ada questioned me and took a sip from her glass.

"He was pushing it quite close, waiting 'til today to tell me it was ready, but I grabbed it earlier. I haven't had the chance to look at it yet. Hopefully, it fits tomorrow morning."

"You should've took some time to yourself to try it on."

"Maybe so, but I don't have the time right now," I replied soon as I heard the front door open and knew it was Honey and Ma.

Honey stopped in the doorway with her yellow Birkin hanging in her hand. Her lips spread from ear to ear as she stood there and looked at the *Congratulations* sign behind me.

"See, y'all be thinking y'all slick." She rested her purse on the table and slipped out her coat. I grabbed the bride sash and draped it over her head.

"I figured spending time with us would've been exactly what you wanted tonight. We got food, games, and drinks. Let the party begin."

Gripping her by the hand, I pulled her further into the living room and we plopped on the huge fluffy pillows that surrounded the coffee table where I had Monopoly set up. Ma grabbed the tray of mixed drinks and brought them over to us. I wasn't a drinker, but I could sip on something fruity.

The night began and honestly, it was cool with it being just us. Honey seemed to be having a great time and that's all that really mattered. Ten o'clock rolled around and Mama Ada and Ma were getting sleepy. We helped them to bed and then Nigel cleaned up our mess. I offered to do it, but he kept telling me that's what he got paid for. Honey and I settled in her bedroom on her bed and sat there talking.

"Are you nervous about tomorrow?"

"Of course, but the crazy thing about it, Law's making it a lil easier to be married to him. He took me on this romantic date the other night and when I tell you, I wanted to jump on the dick..." Honey's mouth slacked, and she fanned herself. "I can only imagine what our wedding night is gon' be like. That's really what I'm nervous about. What if I can't satisfy him like he wants me to?"

"I'm sure he'll probably teach you. All I can say is do the best that you can, but you have to tell me all about it. I wanna know if it really hurts."

Honey snickered. "I will. How's things going with you and Streets?"

"Honey, I really like that man."

"It's crazy how we ended up with brothers."

"It really is."

Honey and I talked for a bit longer before we found ourselves passed out in bed.

CHAPTER FORTY-ONE
STREETS
THAT SAME NIGHT

I sat there in the back of the Escalade, toking on a cigar as I waited for Law to exit the building. He stepped out the door and strolled in my direction. Silently, he climbed into the truck alongside me and asked, "What the fuck is so got damn important that I had to get pulled away from my bachelor party?"

"It's the Giuseppes. I tried to tell them that you were busy, but they weren't taking no for an answer. Their waiting for us at Gold Rosé."

"Are you fucking serious?"

"Yeah."

"Let's get this shit over with, and they better not piss me the fuck off."

The driver pulled off and took us straight to Gold Rosé. When we arrived, it was dark with only a few cars in the parking lot. It was well past closing time since it was going on one in the morning. The only reason they remained open was 'cause of the Giuseppes.

Law and I climbed out of the truck and walked up to the

door. One of the men guarding it opened it for us and we entered. Saint sat there at the table along with Vex. Three other men stood behind them with their guns strapped to 'em.

"Y'all mind telling me why the fuck you pulled me away from my bachelor party? This shit couldn't wait 'til after my fucking wedding?"

"Hello to you too, Law," Saint said with a smile.

The Giuseppes were the other crime family that stayed here in Montgomery. We had the city split straight down the middle. We tried our best to stay the fuck out of each other's way. Every so often, a meeting was called to resolve some shit to try and stop blood from shedding.

"We got a business proposition that we thought would be beneficial for both of us," Saint stated.

"Like I said, this shit couldn't wait 'til after my fucking wedding?"

Saint reached on the floor and dropped a duffel on the table. "Congratulations, nigga. Now can you sit down and hear my fucking proposition?"

Law unzipped the bag and nothing but blue faces stared back at him. Zipping it back up, he handed me the bag. Time was money and Saint understood that. Law sat down at the table and Saint continued. "I came across a new drug. I think it's gon' be major in the city. For a percentage, I'm willing to give you a stake. It's a major money move if you ask me."

"What is this shit?"

Saint reached into his pocket and pulled out a small vial with purple contents. "I call this Lilith. This shit got the fiends going crazy." He handed the drug over to Law. "You can give it a try and see if you like it or not."

"You think I'm that fucking stupid?"

"Or take it with you and have someone else try it. I really don't give a damn."

"What's the percentage?"

"Seventy, thirty. We get seventy and you thirty."

"Nah." Law rolled the vial back in Saint's direction and stood to his feet.

"A'ight, sixty, forty."

"The only way I'm doing this shit is if it's fifty, fifty."

Saint tossed his head back and chuckled. "A'ight. Fifty, fifty." He rolled the drugs back in Law's direction. Law picked it up and slipped it into his pocket.

"I'll get back to you after my wedding, not a moment sooner," he said and strolled toward the door.

"Wait," Saint said behind us, halting Law's strides.

"What now?" he asked when he turned around.

"There's something else you should know."

CHAPTER FORTY-TWO
HONEY
THE WEDDING

The day had come. I was finally about to be Mrs. Lawrence Blanco. I sat there in the bedroom, staring at my dress as it gazed back at me. A knock at the bedroom door grasped my attention. Mama Ada entered with a black box in her hand. "How you feeling?" she asked as she neared where I sat.

"Like my heart is about to burst in my chest."

She giggled. "I thought I should bring you this. It's your something blue." Ada popped the box open, and staring back at me was this gorgeous ass blue sapphire heart pendant necklace. It was so beautiful that I didn't even want to touch it.

"It was my mother's," she said, taking the necklace out the box.

"I can't take this, Mama A."

"You can and you will. You're a part of this family now. You earned your right to have it. Now, turn around so I can put it on." I turned on the edge of the bed and the necklace lay firm against my chest as she clasped it.

"You've been nothing but nice to me ever since I got here.

Thank you."

"You can thank me by giving me plenty of great-grandbabies." Her lips caressed my cheek. "I'm gon' let you get dressed. Do you need any help?"

"No. Coco will be in here any moment. They were finishing up her hair."

"Okay. I'll see you downstairs."

Mama Ada exited the bedroom, and I got up from the bed and went over to the mirror to take a look at the necklace. My fingertips grazed the diamonds around the sapphire. I'd been pulled away from everything I knew and placed in a strange home just to find myself falling for the very monster that ripped me away from my life. Was there something wrong with me? I jumped at the sound of the door opening behind me. Coco stepped into the bedroom dressed in her powder pink robe.

"Sorry it took so long. Are you ready?"

Turning to her, I said, "Tell me I'm making the right decision."

"Honey, I can't tell you that. Only you can make that decision, but if you want to get the hell out of here, I promise I'm gon' be right behind you."

"I think it's a lil too late for that. I'm falling for him."

"Then put on your dress and go out there and get your man."

Another knock at the door interrupted us. Coco pulled the door open and some guy stood there with a dress bag. "Are you Coco?"

"Yes."

"I was told to deliver this to you along with a note." He handed her the bag and note then trotted off.

"What is that?" I questioned her and she shrugged. Coco hung the dress up next to her maid of honor dress and opened the note. "What does it say?" I pried, trying to see what was going on. Her glossy eyes met mine and she flipped the note over where I was able to read it.

Marry me?

If yes, you'll put on this dress I got for you. If I see you in the maid of honor dress, then I know your answer. -Streets

"So what are you gon' do?" I wasn't even mad that he was trying to marry her on my wedding day. Coco and I shared a lot of shit in our lives. Sharing a wedding day would be amazing.

"I don't know. Let me help you get dressed while I think on it."

She unzipped my dress and pulled it from the mannequin. We got mine on then she stood there, gawking at her two dresses. "The decision shouldn't be hard, Coco. If you really like him, then give him a chance. He seems to really make you happy. Don't let another woman end up with him just because you're scared."

Coco stepped to the dress bag and unzipped her dress. It was a gorgeous white mermaid gown. He definitely had been paying attention to her because Coco was a simple girl. Grabbing the dress, she slipped it on and handed me my diamond bouquet then grabbed hers. We exited the bedroom and made our way downstairs where our daddy was waiting for us. When he turned around and saw both of his girls dressed in white, tears filled his eyes.

"I thought I was just giving away one of my girls today, not both of you." He pecked us on the cheek then led us toward the back double doors. The wedding was being hosted in the backyard. They wanted a spring wedding and that's exactly what they got. The tent they rented had strings of pink roses dangling from the ceiling. There was a white runway that led to where the guys were already standing. Daddy escorted Coco down the aisle first and I peeked around, seeing Streets brush the tears from his eyes. Part of him probably thought she'd turn down his gesture, but Coco was a sucker for romance.

Once Coco made it down the aisle, Daddy came back to get me. "Before we go, I just want to say that I'm sorry. I really thought I was doing the right thing at the time. I hate that I took away your life."

"But it worked out for the better, Daddy. I actually like Law."

"I'm glad it did." His lips caressed my cheek and he extended his arm to me. I took it and Teeks' "First Time" began to play. We strolled down the aisle. All eyes were now glued to us. Law stood at the end in his white tux and powder pink shirt. His eyes locked on me, and I swear it was like we were the only ones in the room. I stopped in front of him and Daddy released me. Coco and Streets stood to the left and we stepped to the right of the pastor.

Pastor Grant began to talk and I tuned him out. Law gripped me by the hands and my heart rate kicked up a notch. Standing here in front of him seemed surreal, but this was my new reality.

"I do," I heard Coco say, and it snapped me from my thoughts. The pastor turned to me and Law.

"Lawrence, do you intend to take this woman whose hand you hold to be your lawful wedded wife; and do you pledge before God and man to love, honor, and protect her through sunshine and shadow alike, keeping yourself unto her alone until death shall separate you? If so, answer I do."

Law's eyes searched mine and he replied, "I do," without any hesitation.

"I do," I said before he was even able to ask me, and everyone began to laugh. Gripping him by the collar of his shirt, I pulled him in my direction and collided our lips. Everyone began to whistle and cheer. We pulled apart and faced everyone. Mrs. Lawrence Blanco. Whether I knew it or not, the streets of Montgomery were now legally mine.

We strolled back down the aisle to the door with Coco and Streets behind us. The reception was being held in the ballroom of the house. While everyone piled into the ballroom, Law and I made our way to the front yard to take our wedding photos.

"How does it feel to be stuck with me now?" I asked Law as we neared the front door.

Gripping me by the wrists, he hemmed me against the wall. "When I get my hands on you later, you gon' be begging me to spank that ass." His face nestled in the crook of my neck. "My dick been so hard that the mufucka hurts. I wouldn't even be surprised if you're pregnant in a few weeks." My pussy thumped. The anticipation of finally seeing what it felt like to have sex with him was killing me.

Law released me and we went outside to meet the photographer. Our shoot was short and sweet—straight to the point. By the time we were done, everyone should've been settled in the ballroom.

"I need to use the restroom," I told Law. His phone began to ring. Pulling it out, he looked down at it and said, "Go 'head. I need to take this right quick. Meet me at the ballroom so we can enter together when you're done." Pecking me on the lips, he disappeared down the hallway.

I slipped into the bathroom. It was harder than I thought to pee with that big ass dress, but I finally managed. Once I was done, I washed my hands and exited the bathroom. I was gripped tightly by the wrist. My eyes roamed from the hand up to their face, and it was Wick.

"What the fuck are you doing?" I frowned and tried to snatch from him, but he had a death grip on me. That mufucka had disappeared after Dash's death and that only made what

Law said valid. He had something to do with my brother's death.

"You're coming with me."

"The hell I am." I yanked but he wouldn't release me. Had I pulled any harder, he probably would've pulled my arm from my socket.

"Stop making shit so complicated and just bring yo' ass on," Wick said, tugging me toward the door.

"Did you kill Dash?" Me needing the answer to that question was the only reason why my feet moved behind him.

Stopping in his tracks, he pinched the bridge of his nose then replied, "I told him he should've just minded his own business."

"So you killed him? How could you? You were like a brother to him and you do something like that. You're heartless."

"I did what the fuck I had to do just like he did."

His grip loosened on me and I yanked away from him. Kicking my shoe off, I bent down, grabbed it, and rammed it straight in the side of his neck. Blood gushed. Honestly, I didn't think the shit was gon' work. I snatched his gun from his waistline, kicked him in the stomach, cocked it, and aimed it at his head.

Pow!

A bullet crashed through the center of his forehead, dropping him to the floor.

"I see nothing around here has changed," a woman's voice caught my attention. When I looked up, I saw this woman standing inches away from me. She stood there, looking at Wick's dead body unfazed.

"Who are you?" She looked familiar but I couldn't quite grasp where I'd seen her before.

"Ma?" Law asked, and my heart dropped.

To be continued.

Made in the USA
Columbia, SC
29 May 2025